学术顾问

王　宏　冯智文　李正栓　李丽生　原一川

Academic Advisors
Wang Hong　Feng Zhiwen　Li Zhengshuan
Li Lisheng　　Yuan Yichuan

主　编
李昌银

副主编
黄　瑛　彭庆华

General Editor
Li Changyin
Professor of English Yunnan Normal University

Associate General Editors
Huang Ying
Professor of English Yunnan Normal University

Peng Qinghua
Professor of English Yunnan Normal University

云南少数民族经典作品英译文库
Classics of Yunnan Ethnic Groups in English Translation

主编 李昌银　General Editor　Li Changyin

副主编 黄瑛 彭庆华　Associate General Editors　Huang Ying & Peng Qinghua

Zhaoshutun
召树屯

整理◎岩叠　陈贵培

　　　　刘绮　王松

英译◎吴相如　吴炯

译校◎［美］包琼

Edited by Ai Die, Chen Guipei,
Liu Qi & Wang Song
Translated by Wu Xiangru & Wu Jiong
Revised by Joan Cecile Boulerice

云南出版集团

云南人民出版社

图书在版编目（CIP）数据

召树屯：汉、英 / 岩叠等整理；吴相如，吴炯英
译. -- 昆明：云南人民出版社，2018.12
（云南少数民族经典作品英译文库 / 李昌银主编）
ISBN 978-7-222-17505-1

Ⅰ.①召… Ⅱ.①岩… ②吴… ③吴… Ⅲ.①傣族—
叙事诗—中国—汉、英 Ⅳ.①I222.7

中国版本图书馆CIP数据核字(2018)第277435号

出 品 人	李 维	赵石定
项目统筹	周 祥	殷筱钊
项目组稿	郭木玉	
责任编辑	郭木玉	任建红　李东华
设计制作	马 滨	三人禾
责任校对	李智燕	崔苡菡　付芳侠　周桉吉
责任印制	陆卫华	代隆参

云南少数民族经典作品英译文库
Classics of Yunnan Ethnic Groups in English Translation

召树屯
Zhaoshutun

整理◎岩叠　陈贵培　刘绮　王松
英译◎吴相如　吴炯
译校◎［美］包琼

Edited by Ai Die, Chen Guipei, Liu Qi & Wang Song
Translated by Wu Xiangru & Wu Jiong
Revised by Joan Cecile Boulerice

出 版	云南出版集团　云南人民出版社
发 行	云南人民出版社
社 址	昆明市环城西路609号
邮 编	650034
网 址	www.ynpph.com.cn
E-mail	ynrms@sina.com
开 本	787mm×1092mm　1/16
印 张	11.75
字 数	170千
版 次	2018年12月第1版第1次印刷
印 刷	云南出版印刷（集团）有限责任公司　云南新华印刷一厂
书 号	ISBN 978-7-222-17505-1
定 价	65.00元

云南人民出版社
公众微信号

序 一

◎李正栓

民族典籍英译是传播中国文化、文学和文明的重要途径，是中华文化走出去的重要组成部分。文化与文学的传播，是一个国家提高文化软实力的重要方式，在文化交流和文明建设中起着不可或缺的作用，对提高国家对外话语权、构建国家对外话语体系以及对建设世界文学都有积极意义。

中国各少数民族拥有许多优秀的典籍，具有很高的文物价值、文学价值和文化价值。各民族的先人们通过口头流传或用文字记述了他们各具特色的文化。各少数民族几乎都有自己民族的创世史、史诗和神话传说。

中国民族典籍独具特色，不可替代。重视民族典籍的翻译和研究工作，对于挖掘各民族优秀文化，保护各民族文明，增强各民族之间的沟通和了解，进一步向世界其他地区传播各少数民族优秀文化，乃至提高我国文化软实力都有着重要意义。不少少数民族聚居地处于祖国边疆，有的处在"一带一路"建设关键部位，有的处在与周边国家进行各种交流的重要位置。

中国民族典籍是世界多元文化的有机组成部分，与其他文化共同造就了世界文化的绚丽多姿。世界正因为其文化多样性才变得缤纷多彩。我国各民族典籍中包含的文化多样性极大地丰富了世界多元、特色鲜明的文化。人们对多样性形成全新的认识角度和思维方式。多样性开阔了人们的视野，丰富了人们思考问题的角度。挖掘这些典籍中所蕴含的教育价值和文化价值，对世界其他民族都有指导和借鉴意义，并且有助于建设我国的文化自信。

民族典籍本身蕴含的特殊价值对加强民族文化了解、促进中外文化交流具有重大意义。民族典籍英译具有文学翻译和文化传递之功能，有对外宣传作用，还是一种文学外交。因此，民族典籍翻译和研究对于维护祖国统一、促进民族团结、稳定边疆以及增强国内各民族和中外文化之间的交流都起着极为重要的作用。

中华人民共和国成立以后，中央政府一直十分重视民族典籍翻译和研究工作，提供了强有力的政策支持，并采取了一系列有效措施，加快了各少数民族典籍的抢救、整理、翻译和研究的进程。中央政府多次召开西藏工作会议和新疆工作会议。近年来，国际和国内对于多元文化高度关注，少数民族文学典籍的翻译已然成为业内研究的热点。

近年来，民族典籍翻译和研究迅猛发展，势头良好。国家大力支持，发放国家社科基金课题，教育部和国家民委也发放课题，扶持了一大批研究者。很多民族典籍翻译课题得以立项并顺利开展；为数不少的民族典籍被翻译成汉语、英语和其他语言并出版发行；越来越多的业界人士致力于这个满富生机的学术领域。

在中国文化走出去的国家战略下，全国少数民族典籍英译学术研讨会陆续召开，已经召开三次。

云南是中国民族最多的省份。人口在 5000 人以上的少数民族有 25 个，其中有 15 个民族为云南所特有，分别是：白族、哈尼族、傣族、傈僳族、佤族、拉祜族、纳西族、景颇族、布朗族、普米族、阿昌族、基诺族、怒族、德昂族、独龙族。其中除白族人口占全国白族人口总数的 84% 以上外，其他 14 个民族 95% 居住在云南。

云南还是我国跨境民族最多的省份。在云南的 25 个少数民族中，有 16 个民族跨境而居，分别是：傣族、壮族、苗族、景颇族、瑶族、哈尼族、德昂族、佤族、拉祜族、彝族、阿昌族、傈僳族、布依族、怒族、布朗族、独龙族。

云南少数民族创造了辉煌的文化。据不完全统计，云南少数民族文字文献古籍蕴藏量达 10 万余册（卷），口传古籍 4 万余种。云南省民委少数民族古籍整理出版规划办公室为了挽救和保护这些古籍，计划在 5 年内编纂出版 100 卷《云南少数民族古籍珍本集成》。这是一个令人瞩目的庞大计划。将这些古籍中的珍品翻译介绍给世界，不仅能够弘扬云南省丰富多彩的民族文化，而且有助于增进与南亚东南亚国家的理解与交流，为"一带一路"倡议的实施做出贡献。

云南师范大学外国语学院很重视这一领域的工作。在外国语学院领导支持下，李昌银教授带领一个由教授和中青年学者组成的团队对精选出来的 17 部云南少数民族经典作品进行英译，计划在 5 年内（"十三五"期间）翻译出版。这是一项十分有意义的宏大工程。

这 17 部民族典籍，内容全部为各民族的英雄史诗或神话传说，具有很高的历史意义和文学价值。这些作品涉及阿昌族、白族、傣族、德昂族、哈尼族、景颇族、拉祜族、苗族、纳西族、普米族、彝族等 11 个少数民族。

云南师范大学这支翻译队伍实力强大，主要由一些多年从事翻译教学、研究和实践的教授和副教授组成，他们是李昌银、黄瑛、彭庆华、孙兴文、吴相如、刘德周、杨慧芳、郜菊、陈萍、包琼（Joan Boulerice）等国内外专家学者。他们在云南翻译界都是风云人物。

在民族典籍英译中，这支队伍异军突起，为我国民族典籍英译壮大了声势，必将为中国民族典籍走向世界而成为世界文学的一部分做出新贡献。

民族典籍翻译与研究事业关乎国家的稳定统一，关乎民族关系的和谐发展，关乎世界多元文化的实现。在中国，民族典籍资源极为丰富，有待进一步挖掘、翻译。因此，民族典籍英译前景光明。同时，我们也应意识到，仍有许多濒临消失的少数民族典籍亟待拯救，民族典籍翻译与研究工作任重而道远。

（李正栓，中国英汉语比较研究会典籍英译专业委员会常务副会长兼秘书长）

Foreword by Li Zhengshuan

The translation of Chinese ethnic classics is an important approach in spreading Chinese culture, literature and civilization. It is a crucial component of Chinese culture going global. The spreading of Chinese culture and literature is a national policy and an important way to improve the cultural soft power of China. It plays an indispensable role in the cultural exchange between China and other countries and the development of world literature.

The ethnic groups in China have countless excellent classics with high anthropological, literary and cultural value. The ancestors of each ethnic group have passed down their distinctive culture orally or in writing. Almost all the ethnic groups have their own story of creation, epics, myths and legends.

Chinese ethnic classics are unique and irreplaceable. It is imperative to attach importance to the translation and research of ethnic classics; to explore the excellent ethnic cultures; to protect the civilization of ethnic groups; to enhance the communication and understanding among ethnic groups; to further spread the outstanding culture of ethnic groups to other parts of the world; and to build the cultural strength of China. Many ethnic groups live in the border areas and thus play an important role in the cultural and economic cooperation between China and its neighbors in the context of the Belt and Road Initiative.

Chinese ethnic classics are an important component of the magnificence and diversity of world culture. It is diversity that makes the world so colorful. The cultural diversity of Chinese ethnic classics has greatly enriched the world's pluralism and its distinctive features. People around the world have formed a new understanding of diversity. This diversity has expanded people's horizon and enriched their way of thinking. Digging out the educational and cultural value in these classics can contribute to the construction of China's self-confidence in culture.

The special value of the ethnic classics itself is of great significance to the strengthening of national culture and intercultural communication between China and foreign countries. The translation of ethnic classics is not just a literary exchange, but also a form of cultural communication. It is diplomacy through literature in that it consolidates the cultural ties between China and other countries.

After the founding of the People's Republic of China, the central government attached great importance to the translation and research of ethnic classics, provided the a great deal of policy support, and adopted a series of effective measures to speed up the process of rescuing, collating, translating and studying ethnic classics. The central government has convened several working conferences on Tibet and Xinjiang. In recent years, both China and other countries have paid close attention to multiculture. The translation of ethnic classics has become a hot topic.

In recent years, the translation and research of ethnic classics have progressed rapidly and have shown good prospects. The government strongly supports and grants the research projects of the national social science fund. The Ministry of Education and the State Ethnic Affairs Commission are also issuing research projects and giving funding to a large number of researchers. Many research projects on ethnic classics have been approved and carried out. Many ethnic classics have been translated into Chinese, English and other languages and published. More and more professionals have dedicated themselves to this new sphere of learning.

In this context, the academic conferences on translation of ethnic classics are held one after another all around the country. And up to now three have been held.

Yunnan is the province which has the most ethnic groups in China. Besides Han people, there are 25 ethnic groups, each with a population of more than 5,000. Among them, 15 ethnic groups are unique to Yunnan, which are the Bai, the Hani, the Dai, the Lisu, the Wa, the Lahu, the Naxi, the Jingpo, the Bulang, the Pumi, the Achang, the Jinuo, the Nu, the De'ang and the Dulong. Among these, 84% of the total number of the Bai people in China and 95% of the other 14 ethnic groups are living in Yunnan.

Yunnan is also the province which has the most cross-border ethnic groups. Of the 25 ethnic groups, 16 live across the border, namely: the Dai, the Zhuang, the Miao, the Jingpo, the Yao, the Hani, the De'ang, the Wa, the Lahu, the Yi, the Achang, the Lisu, the Buyi, the Nu, the Bulang and the Dulong.

The ethnic groups in Yunnan have created splendid cultures. According to statistics, the number of classics of Yunnan ethnic groups is more than 100 thousand volumes and classics in oral tradition are more than 40 thousand. In order to save and protect these ancient books, the Office of Classics Collation and Publishing of Yunnan Ethnic Groups Affairs Commission planned to compile and publish 100 volumes of *A Collection of Yunnan Ethnic Group Rare Books* in five years, which is an ambitious plan. The introduction of the ancient classics via translation can not only promote and develop the colorful ethnic cultures of Yunnan, but also contribute to the understanding and exchange between China and countries in South Asia and Southeast Asia and to the implementation of the Belt and Road Initiative as well.

The School of Foreign Languages and Literature of Yunnan Normal University is paying close attention to this field. With the support of the School and the University, Professor Li Changyin is leading a group of professors and young scholars to do the project of *"Classics of Yunnan Ethnic Groups in English Translation"*, which includes 17 ethnic classics selected carefully from Yunnan's bountiful ethnic classics. These books are the heroic epics or myths and legends of each ethnic groups with great historical significance and literary value. They will finish the translation in five years (during "the thirteenth five-year plan"). After that, all the works will be published by Yunnan People's Publishing House.

The 17 works cover 11 ethnic groups: the Achang, the Bai, the Dai, the De'ang, the Hani, the Jingpo, the Lahu, the Miao, the Naxi, the Pumi and the Yi. All of these groups except the Miao and the Yi are unique to Yunnan.

The translation team of Yunnan Normal University is full of strength and vitality, composed of professors and associate professors who have been occupied in translation teaching, research, and practice for a long time. They are Li Changyin, Huang Ying, Peng Qinghua, Sun Xingwen, Wu Xiangru, Liu Dezhou, Yang Huifang, Gao Ju, Chen Ping, Joan Boulerice and other experts and scholars who are representative figures in the translation field in Yunnan province.

This team is a new force that has suddenly arisen in terms of translating ethnic classics. It is expanding the momentum of ethnic classics translation in China and has made a new contribution for China's ethnic classics to go global and become a part of world literature.

The translation and research of ethnic classics are related

to the development of Chinese culture and the realization of multiculturalism in the world. In China, ethnic classics are extremely rich in resources, which require us to make further exploration and research and translate them into other languages. Therefore, the future of translating ethnic classics is bright. At the same time, we should also realize that there are still many ethnic works which are close to extinction and urgently need to be rescued. We still have a long way to go in the fields of translation and research in ethnic classics.

(Li Zhengshuan, Standing Vice Chairman and Secretary General, Classics Translation Committee of CACSEC)

序 二

◎王　宏

　　好友云南师范大学外国语学院李昌银教授来电嘱托我为"云南少数民族经典作品英译文库"的出版写一序言，并随即发来该文库的背景资料，让我"不着急，慢慢写"。我本人从事中国典籍英译及研究，深知少数民族典籍对外传译的重要性，但又是少数民族典籍翻译的门外汉。因此，我是怀着虚心学习的态度来写此序言的。近年来，在中国文化"走出去"战略工程大背景下，在中央和地方各级政府的大力支持下，我国少数民族典籍的对外传译及研究工作顺利开展，取得了很大的进步。请看以下数据：

　　2008 年，广西百色学院韩家权教授获批国家社科基金项目《布洛陀史诗》（壮汉英对照）。该项目已顺利结项，并于 2013 年 12 月获得中国民间文艺最高奖"山花奖"。

　　2012 年，广西百色学院外语系翻译团队翻译的国家级非物质文化遗产《壮族嘹歌》（英文版）由广西师范大学出版社正式出版。

　　2012 年，东北大学秦皇岛分校吴松林教授主编的《蒙古族系列：江格尔（汉英对照）》（上下册）由吉林大学出版社出版。

　　2013 年，河北师范大学李正栓教授英译《藏族格言诗》

由长春出版社出版发行。

2013 年，云南财经大学崔晓霞教授撰写的《〈阿诗玛〉英译研究》收入由王宏印教授主编、民族出版社出版的"民族典籍翻译研究丛书"。

2014 年，东北大学秦皇岛分校吴松林教授撰写的《满族档案文献研究》申请到国家社科后期资助，他英译的《英雄格斯尔可汗》由吉林大学出版社出版。

2014 年，中南民族大学张立玉教授主持的"土家族主要典籍英译及研究"获批国家社科基金项目。

2015 年，西安外国语大学梁真惠副教授撰写的《〈玛纳斯〉翻译传播研究》收入由王宏印教授主编、民族出版社出版的"民族典籍翻译研究丛书"。

与此同时，第一届和第二届全国少数民族典籍英译学术研讨会分别于 2012 年和 2014 年在广西民族大学和大连民族学院举行，参加会议的院校分布之广、与会代表数量之众、提交论文数量之多和涉及研究话题之细，十分可喜。2016 年还将在中南民族大学举行第三届全国少数民族典籍英译学术研讨会。

为什么少数民族典籍的对外传译及研究工作在短短几年就受到译界的青睐，取得众多成果？我认为，这在很大程度上归于典籍翻译界乃至翻译界同仁对"中国典籍"的重新思考和认识。中国典籍浩如烟海，卷帙浩繁，举世瞩目，是全人类共同的精神财富。但对于中国典籍的理解，我们以前较多限于汉民族的重要文献和书籍，而对少数民族多有忽略。在讨论中国典籍时，也较多关注古代文学作品。其实，中国典籍指"中国清代末年1911年以前的重要文献和书籍"，这就要求我们从事典籍翻译时，不但要翻译古代文学典籍作品，还要翻译古代哲学、科技、法律、医学、经济、军事、天文、地理等诸多方面的典籍作品，不但要翻译汉民族的典籍作品，也要翻译各少数民族的典籍作品。

民族典籍具有该民族的原型符号的特质，蕴藏着能够"遗传"并不断"再生"的文化基因。民族典籍是中华传统文化的内核，同时还是中华传统文化的符号构成规则。中国是具有56个民族的多民族国家，少数民族典籍是我国少数民族勤劳与智慧的结晶，是中华文明、也是世界文明不可或缺的一部分。少数民族典籍对外传译具有跨文化交流的作用，它不但有助于更多的人了解少数民族的独特文化，而且还有助于保护少数民族文化的独特性、维持少数民族文化多样性、促进各民族团结、提升中华文化软实力等。

中国少数民族典籍涉及宗教、文学、历史、语言、医学、天文历算等领域，内容丰富，版本多样，载体特殊，传承奇特。仅以《中国少数民族古籍总目提要》为例，该书于1997年正式立项，全书总体设计约60卷、110册，目前已出版23个民族卷共20册：纳西族卷、白族卷、东乡族卷·裕固族卷·保安族卷、土族卷·撒拉族卷、锡伯族卷、哈尼族卷、回族卷·铭刻、柯尔克孜族卷、羌族卷、毛南族卷·京族卷、仫佬族卷、达斡尔族卷、土家族卷、鄂温克族卷、鄂伦春族卷、赫哲族卷、苗族卷、侗族卷、黎族卷、朝鲜族卷。该书真实地反映了我国各少数民族古籍赋存的全面情况，充实了中国的历史和文化内容，为后人探索各种文化形式的源流、揭示中国社会文化发展的轨迹提供了极为珍贵的资料，为我国乃至世界各国人文科学研究提供了一套新颖而全面的资料，对于弘扬中华民族传统文化具有深远的历史意义和现实意义。

少数民族典籍的对外传译是一项艰巨的工作，涉及将少数民族语言译成汉语、少数民族语言之间的互译和少数民族语言译成外语（主要是英语）。前两类翻译历史源远流长，最早可追溯到春秋战国时代《越人歌》的翻译，即汉、壮语之间的翻译。少数民族典籍译成外语的时间则要晚一些。据考证，维吾尔族古典长诗《福乐智慧》成书于 1069 年或 1070 年，目前尚未发现完整的原稿，只存留下来三个抄本，分别为赫拉特抄本、费尔干纳抄本与埃及抄本，其中费尔干纳抄本于 12~13 世纪用阿拉伯文纳斯赫体抄写，1914 年发现于今中亚乌孜别克斯坦纳曼干城，现存于该共和国科学院东方研究所。这是少数民族典籍译介到国外的最早纪录。少数民族典籍外译在现代有了较快发展。一些少数民族典籍，如藏族的《格萨尔王传》、蒙古族的《江格尔》和柯尔克孜族的《玛纳斯》等英雄史诗，云南彝族的《阿诗玛》、维吾尔族的《艾里甫和赛乃姆》等民间叙事长诗已先后被翻译成英语及其他外国文字，为世人所知。这对传承少数民族经典，推动中外文化交流起到了不可替代的作用。然而，还有大量的中国少数民族典籍等待我们去翻译和研究。

云南省少数民族典籍资源十分丰富。据不完全统计，云南少数民族文字文献古籍蕴藏量达 10 万余册（卷），口传古籍 4 万余种。"云南少数民族经典作品英译文库"正是依托云南省丰富的少数民族典籍资源，借助云南师范大学外国语学院强大的翻译师资队伍，在云南人民出版社的有力支持下，首次将云南少数民族经典作品成系列对外译介的大力举措。云南师范大学外国语学院对"云南少数民族经典作品英译文库"十分重视，他们首先邀请省内外少数民族语言文化研究专家对云南民族典籍和民族文化经典作品进行筛选，做到"好中选好，优中选优"，同时调配最强的翻译力量承担文库的翻译任务。我粗略看了该文库的选题，发现选题面广，覆盖范围宽，收入了云南省阿昌族、白族、傣族、纳西族、德昂族、哈尼族、景颇族、拉祜族、苗族、普米族和彝族等民族的典籍作品。云南共有25个少数民族，其中11个少数民族的典籍作品都覆盖到了，不少作品还是首次译成英文。这将彻底改变云南少数民族典籍由于对外译介数量较少，不为世界了解的尴尬局面。

对于云南师范大学外国语学院而言，把少数民族典籍英译作为翻译专业的优势特色进行建设，这将对该院的学科建设起到助推作用。"云南少数民族经典作品英译文库"所产生的翻译成果和研究成果将培养出一批优秀的典籍翻译和研究团队，凸显该院在全国的学术特色和学术影响，同时还能将翻译能力和研究能力转化为教学能力，提高云南师范大学外国语学院翻译专业研究生的培养质量，为社会输送高水平的翻译人才，有力地支撑学院翻译专业学科的建设和发展。我对云南师范大学外国语学院的翻译师资队伍较为熟悉。作为云南省唯一获得省级高校优势特色学科建设项目的外国语学院，该院具有雄厚的翻译师资力量，在云南省各高校中当属第一。多年来，该院翻译与跨文化研究团队一直承担着对外交流与合作的各种口笔译项目及任务。由外国语学院精心挑选和确定的"云南少数民族经典作品英译文库"翻译人员绝大多数都是云南省翻译领域里的知名教授或专家，有国外留学经历，且具有扎实的英汉双语语言功底，曾翻译出版多部译著和翻译作品，并且主持和参与过多项翻译项目的研究。我阅读李昌银教授发来的文库翻译人员名单，发现多名我所熟悉的知名教授、博士也在其中，感到格外放心。

"云南少数民族经典作品英译文库"的出版发行是云南省翻译界的一件大事，也是我国少数民族典籍翻译传来的又一佳音。想当年，我和《大中华文库》总协调人李林老师曾在参加全国典籍英译学术研讨会之余一起找到李昌银教授，敦促李教授向学校和同事呼吁，少数民族典籍翻译及研究是富矿，值得快挖、深挖，能早出成果，出大成果。今天，我们当年的心愿变成了美好的现实，心里感到特别高兴。再次热烈祝贺"云南少数民族经典作品英译文库"的顺利出版！

（王宏，中国典籍翻译研究会副会长、苏州大学博士生导师）

Foreword by Wang Hong

My friend Professor Li Changyin of Yunnan Normal University asked me to write a few words for the publication of *Classics of Yunnan Ethnic Groups in English Translation*. I am more than delighted to do it. As I have been doing research in the English translation of Chinese classics, I know how important his work is. In recent years, substantial progress has been made in translating Chinese ethnic classics into English and other foreign languages. Books published in this respect include *The Liao Songs of the Zhuang Nationality* (Nanning: Guangxi Normal University Press, 2008, English Edition), *Mongolian Series: Jianggeer* (Changchun: Jilin University Press, 2012, Bilingual Edition), *Tibetan Gnomic Verses Translated into English* (Changchun: Changchun Press, 2013), and *Geser Khan: a Hero* (Changchun: Jilin University Press, 2014). Several projects in the English translation of ethnic classics have received funding from the National Planning Office of Philosophy and Social Science and, as a result, a number of monographs and PhD dissertations have been published.

Meanwhile, it is encouraging to see that the first conferences on English translation of ethnic classics in China have been held in Guangxi Nationalities University and

Dalian Nationalities Institute respectively. Participants were both many and enthusiastic. Many papers were presented and a lot of topics discussed. The third conference will be hosted by South Central Nationalities University in 2016.

Why, then, has this field attracted so much attention from translators and scholars alike and accomplished so much in just a few years? The answer, I believe, lies in a rethinking of what constitutes Chinese classics as an indispensable part of human heritage. We used to see Chinese classics as more or less equal to the classics of the Han people, excluding works by other ethnic groups. Moreover, when we talk about Chinese classics, we focus too much on the literary works of ancient times. Yet Chinese classics actually refer to "important works and books before 1911, the year when the Qing dynasty fell, bringing an end to imperial rule." This definition requires us to pay attention not just to literary works, but also writings in other subjects, such as philosophy, science, law, medicine, economics, military affairs, astronomy, and geography, not only Han works, but writings by other ethnic groups as well.

The classical works of a nation are its archetypal symbols, the major carriers of its cultural genes. Chinese classics make up the core of Chinese tradition. The Chinese nation consists of 56 ethnic groups. Ethnic classics are an important part of not only Chinese traditional culture, but also of world civilization. The translation of these works into other languages is important in that it helps to promote cross-cultural communications between China and other countries and to protect and preserve the uniqueness and diversity of ethnic cultures by making them accessible to foreign readers.

Chinese ethnic classics cover a variety of areas, such as religion, literature, history, language, medicine, astrology, and calendar, with numerous editions, special media and unique ways of transmission from generation to generation. Take, for example, *An Anthology of Chinese Ethnic Classics*, a colossal project that includes 110 volumes, 20 of which, from 23 ethnic groups, have been published. The anthology reflects the variety and quantity of China's ethnic classics and provides valuable material and resources for studying, understanding and developing Chinese culture and history in a more comprehensive and sustainable way.

The translation of Chinese ethnic classics into foreign languages is a very demanding job, involving rendering from ethnic languages to Chinese, between ethnic languages, and from ethnic languages (often via Chinese) to foreign languages. The first two types of translation can be traced back to the Spring and Autumn Period, when *The Song of the Yue People* was translated from their mother tongue into Chinese. The earliest translation of ethnic classics into a foreign language is *Wisdom of Royal Glory*, a long poem of the Uygurs, which was rendered from the source language into Arabic and is now in the Oriental Institute of Uzbekistan at Namangan. But it was not until modern times that the translation of ethnic classics into foreign languages accelerated. Noticeably, ethnic epics, such as *The Story of Prince Geser* of the Tibetans, *The Story of Jianggeer* of the Mongolians, *Manas* of the Kyrgyz, and narrative poems such as *Ashima* of the Yi people, *Alip and Salam* of the Uygurs, etc., have been published. These translations have contributed to acquainting the world with Chinese ethnic classics, but many remain to be translated.

Yunnan is rich in ethnic classics, boasting more than 100 thousand volumes of written classics and over 40 thousand pieces of oral literature. Relying on such bountiful resources, as a collective endeavor of the translation team of the School of Foreign Languages and Literature, Yunnan Normal University and with the help of Yunnan People's Publishing House, *Classics of Yunnan Ethnic Groups in English Translation* is the first project to translate Yunnan ethnic classics into English on a large scale. The School adheres to a professional spirit and academic standard in carrying out the project by selecting the most authoritative texts in the source language (Chinese) and recruiting the best translators from its huge faculty. The selection of the works, covering eleven of the twenty-five ethnic groups of the province, indicates expertise and insight. The implementation of the project will change the embarrassing obscurity of Yunnan ethnic classics by making them known to the world, many of them for the first time.

In light of disciplinary development, the project is of

great importance, too. Participating in the translation will strengthen the academic foundation of the teachers, enrich their experience and enhance their translation skills and research ability. This in turn will help them become better teachers and thus able to educate students with higher quality. The publication of the books will add greatly to the faculty accomplishments of the School and raise the academic standing of Yunnan Normal University by taking the first step in this direction among the universities of Yunnan province.

This publication project is a great event not only for Yunnan itself, but also for China. Looking back, I remember that Professor Li Changyin, our friend Li Lin, editor of the *Library of Chinese Classics*, and I talked enthusiastically about initiating something like this in Yunnan when we attended a conference on the translation of ethnic classics in Soochow. Lin and I strongly suggested that Professor Li do it as soon as possible. Now I am very pleased to see our talk becoming reality. Again, my congratulations on the publication of *Classics of Yunnan Ethnic Groups in English Translation*!

（Wang Hong, PhD supervisor at Soochow University, Vice Chairman of Classics Translation Committee of CACSEC）

General Introduction

This publication project, Classics of *Yunnan Ethnic Groups in English Translation*, aims at introducing Yunnan ethnic classical works to the world by making them available to native speakers of English who might be interested in them. With the publication of the *Library of Chinese Classics*, which consists only of books written by Han authors in classical Chinese, attention now is being turned to the English translation and publication of ethnic classics, books produced by ethnic writers about their history and culture. Universities in provinces such as Guangxi, Guizhou, Liaoning, Xinjiang, and Xizang, have taken the initiative. We in Yunnan must do something, because Yunnan has the largest number of ethnic groups in China. 15 of the 25 ethnic groups in the province, the Bai, the Dai, the Hani, the Lisu, the Wa, the Lahu, the Naxi, the Jingpo, the Bulang, the Pumi, the Achang, the Jinuo, the Nu, the De'ang, and the Dulong, live in no other place but Yunnan. The classics of these people, either in their own languages or in Chinese translations, are a great treasure house, which should be accessible to English readers and scholars. But what works should be translated first?

All the 25 ethnic groups in Yunnan have their classics, epics, mythology, creation stories, folksongs, folk drama, mountain songs, and funeral lament lyrics, most of which exist in different versions in different places. According to one estimation, there are more than 100 thousand volumes of them, excluding those in oral form. After a thorough survey and extensive consultations with experts of ethnic studies, we concluded that priority must be given to epics and mythologies, as they reflect an ethnic people's philosophy, history and culture more than anything else by narrating the stories of where and how they think they came from. From many epics and mythologies, we selected 17 of the most authoritative and popular classics representing 11 Yunnan ethnic groups, the Yi, the Bai, the Miao, the Hani, the Lahu, the Naxi, the Jingpo, the Pumi, the Achang, the Dai, and the De'ang. These works are all in Chinese, translated from the original by bilingual scholars whose mother tongue is their own ethnic language and who are fluent and proficient in Chinese. Some were recorded from their oral form at rituals and performances. We did not choose texts written in the ethnic language, not least because it is very hard to find a translator who is skilled in both the ethnic language and English. Moreover, some of the classics in the ethnic language were circulated in various oral forms and fragments. The published Chinese versions have been carefully edited and translated, hence they are more reliable. The next question is: how to translate them?

It happens that all of the 17 works except one are in

verse form, with lines more or less the same length and loose rhymes, but no regular meter. A poem must be rendered into a poem; anything less is unacceptable. So here are the general rules we follow when doing the translation.

One. If the original is verse, the translated text must be verse, too.

Two. Reproduce the ideas and the images of the original as completely as possible.

Three. Reproduce the figures of speech of the original as much as possible.

Four. Do not change the number of lines in a stanza unless absolutely necessary.

Five. Do not use standard meters in English, because the Chinese original does not follow any regular meter. Use the natural rhythm of English instead, but most of the lines should look more or less the same length.

Six. Do not use rhyme unless it comes naturally and is faithful to the content of the original.

What we try to do is, to use Susan Bassnett's words, "transplant the seed", not the tree itself. As for the various aspects of form, particularly meter and end rhyme, we reproduce them when it is possible and abandon them when it is necessary.

Who will do the translations? As this is a collective project of the School of Foreign Languages and Literature of Yunnan Normal University, our team consists of a dozen faculty members and two students from our MA translation program who are already teachers in other universities. All the translators have been teaching translation and doing translation research for a long time. They have published not just academic articles on translation, but also translated books from English to Chinese or vice versa.

Traditionally, people translate into their mother tongue, not into a foreign language. But the situation is changing. Many translators today are translating from their mother tongue into a foreign language. The quality can be good, as Nike K. Pokorn and Stuart Campbell prove in *Challenging the Traditional Axioms*: *Translation into a non-mother tongue* (Amsterdam: John Benjamins Publishing Company, 2005) and *Translation into the Second Language* (New York: Routledge, 2013) respectively. The case of China provides further evidence for their argument. The translation of Chinese classics into English was initiated by James Legge and Herbert Allen Giles in the 19th century and carried on in the 20th century by Arthur Waley, David Hawkes, Burton Watson, John Minford, Stephen Owen and others. It is noticeable that these English and American sinologists were soon joined by Chinese scholars residing in the West, such as Hongming (Tomson) Gu and Lin Yutang, among others. They took up the job because they thought it was their obligation to give English readers more faithful translations than Western sinologists could, who, as their target language is their mother tongue, often misinterpret the original text and misrepresent Chinese culture. Since the 1950s, there has been an increasingly powerful trend for Mainland Chinese translators to render or re-render Chinese classics into foreign languages, English in particular. In our time, this work is gathering momentum, enthusiastically advocated and actively practiced by such well-known translation experts as Yang Xianyi of Beijing Foreign Language Press, Xu Yuanchong of Beijing University, Wang Rongpei of Dalian Foreign Language Institute, Wang Hongyin of Nankai University, Wang Hong of Soochow University, Li Zhengshuan of Hebei Normal University, and many more. These professors are not just translators, but also scholars in translation studies. More importantly, some of them, Xu Yuanchong, Wang Hong and Li Zhengshuan, for example, have had their translations published by Western publishers, which suggests that their English meets the international standard.

In the case of our project, we request that the translators do their best to produce good translations. When they submit them to us, they should represent the highest level that they can attain. Then the general editors appointed by the School read the translated texts and remove inaccurate renderings and grammar mistakes if there are any. On top of that, we've taken an indispensable measure to ensure that our English is readable. We asked Ms. Joan Cecile Boulerice, an American teacher who has been teaching English in our school since

2009, to read every text that we've translated and improve the English by making it more natural and idiomatic. This is the best we can do. Of course any problems that still remain in the translations are ours. They have nothing to do with our American teacher.

As the project is well under way, we would like to thank all those who have helped to make it possible. Ms Guo Muyu, director of the South and Southeast Asia Editorial Department, Yunnan People's Publishing House, has been most helpful in our cooperation. In addition, she has added importance to the project by turning it into a national publication project. Yunnan Normal University has supported us by paying the publication fees so that the translators won't have to be burdened with the financial responsibilities for this project. Professor Li Zhengshuan and Professor Wang Hong not only have always encouraged us to go on but have also written the forewords for the project, putting it in a global perspective. Ms Joan Boulerice's revision has ensured the fluency of the translated texts. Finally, special thanks must be given to Professor Wang Hong, again, and Mr Li Lin of Hunan People's Press for their suggestion that has helped us conceive the project from the very beginning.

(The General Editors, School of Foreign Languages & Literature, Yunnan Normal University, Kunming)

A Brief Introduction to *Zhaoshutun*

Zhaoshutun (also called *Zhaoshutun and Nanmunuona*), a secular folktale, is one of the most renowned classics of the Dai ethnic group in China. It is derived from *Pattra-leaf Scripture*, a Buddhist scripture. *Zhaoshutun* is a narrative poem widely read in Xishuangbanna, Simao, Dehong and some other Dai communities in China and in Southeast Asian countries. In 2008, *Zhaoshutun and Nanmunuona* was included in the second batch of The National List of the Intangible Cultural Heritage of China. *Zhaoshutun* is the first literary work of the Dai ethnic group that has been translated from the Dai language into Chinese.

Zhaoshutun is a narrative poem, collected and edited by Ai Die and other scholars, and published by Yunnan People's Publishing House. It tells the fabulous story of Dai Prince Zhaoshutun falling in love with the youngest daughter of the Peacock Kingdom and the two lovers undergoing hardship and eventually getting married. The whole poem contains twelve cantos: The Song of a Poet; Prince Zhaoshutun; Seven Princesses in Mengdongban; The Hunter; Farewell; Love; The Rite of Tying a Thread; The War; The Disaster; The Chase; Arriving at Mengdongban; and Reunion. Like all fairy tales, the prince and the princess lived happily ever after.

The Translators

目 录

Contents

第一章　诗人的歌

Canto 1　The Song of a Poet

太阳从树林里伸出头

呆呆地望着我写这个故事

公鸡也朝我扇开翅膀

我的故事正在金色的天空中飞翔

美丽的故事像一片艳丽的彩霞

纯洁的爱情就像并蒂开放的鲜花

真心相爱的青年人啊

请把这份礼物收下

我要用最诚实的心

描下他们的欢乐和痛苦

让我的歌啊

像一棵绿莹莹的菩提树

请四面八方飞来的鸟群

都停下翅膀

请会唱的"鹋托朗"①

绕着菩提树歌唱

从远方来的客人

带来他们的歌声

---

① 鹋托朗：是一种在夜里唱歌的鸟，声音婉转动人。

Right from the forest the sun rose,

And stared at me writing the tale.

The rooster spread its wings.

My tale was flying in the golden air.

The tale was as beautiful as a rosy cloud.

The love was as pure as twin flowers

On one stalk, a gift was prepared

For the young couple, true love possessors.

I'd like to portray their joy and sorrow

With my sincere heart.

Let my song grow

Like a green pipal tree.

I'll ask birds to come from far and near

To fold their wings here.

I'll invite Nuotuolang[①]

To sing songs round the pipal tree.

The guests coming from afar

Will bring their songs here.

---

① Nuotuolang is a bird that likes singing at night, and her voice sounds like a sweet melody.

使各村各寨来的男女
带来他们的爱情

常青的菩提树啊
每一片叶子都是有情人的心
那蒙蒙的大雾啊
它夜夜来滋润

Men and women coming from villages near and far

Will bring in their love and care.

The pipal tree will remain green forever,

Each leaf is the heart of a lover.

The ocean of mist

Will moisten everything here every night.

第二章 王子召树屯

Canto 2　Prince Zhaoshutun

在古老的勐板加地方

住着皇后玛茜娜

她梦见老鹰落在屋顶上

过了十个月，生下了一个男孩

为了孩子的命运

国王请来了"摩古拉"①

摩古拉翻开了历书

在四十六个格子②里寻找幸福

"天空中最能飞的是老鹰

地上跑得最快的是金鹿

孩子的名字啊

应该叫作'召树屯'③

"最好看的玉石常常有斑痕

生得最直的树容易遭受风吹雨淋

幸福的王子

他会遭到爱情的折腾"

---

① 摩古拉是傣族卜卦算命的人。
② 四十六个格子：是傣族卜卦算命的根据，在傣族经书中相传有四十六种野兽，前一种野兽管辖后一种。
③ 召树屯意即坚强勇敢的王子。

There was an ancient place called Mengbanjia,

Where Queen Maxina used to live,

Once she dreamed of an eagle landing on the rooftop.

Ten months later, she gave birth to a baby boy.

To secure a good destiny for the prince,

The King called Mogula① in.

Mogula opened an almanac,

And searched for happiness in 46 checks②.

　"The eagle is the king of birds in the air,

The golden deer is the fastest runner on the ground.

The name of the prince

Should be Zhaoshutun③."

"We all know that there are black spots on the best jade,

The straight tree is easily exposed to rain and wind.

The happy prince will go through ups and downs

When it comes to the matter of love."

---

① Mogula: an augur, who could interpret omens according to an almanac in the Dai culture.

② In the legend, Mogula cast someone's fortune on the basis of the 46 checks. There were forty-six kinds of animals in the almanac. Each animal controls the one that follows it.

③ Zhaoshutun: the prince in Mengbanjia, a man of strong will.

十六年的幼苗长成树

十六年的召树屯长成英俊的青年

他的容貌像熔金般闪光

他的心肠像麂子般善良

他像一条神龙

在勐板加地方造下湖水

勐板加的百姓

就像开在湖里的金莲

英俊的召树屯

常常骑着马带着弩箭

在森林里追逐金鹿

在高空中射落飞雁。

他也按照风俗

领着百姓赕佛①

祈求"灭巴拉②"

给勐板加带来风调雨顺

---

① 赕佛：即献佛、敬佛之意。
② 灭巴拉是管理雨水的神。

In sixteen years, the seedlings grew into a big tree.

In sixteen years, the prince grew into a handsome young man,

His appearance, as glittering as the molten gold,

His heart, as kind as a muntjac.

Like a dragon,

He created a lake in Mengbanjia

Where the people were

Like the blooming golden lotuses.

The handsome Zhaoshutun

Used to ride a horse with an arrow in his hand,

And chase a golden deer in the forest,

Or shoot down the flying geese in the air.

Based on the old custom,

He led people to hold the Danfo[1] ceremony

To pray to Miebala[2]

For good weather in Mengbanjia.

---

[1] Danfo: a religious practice, a way of worshipping or showing respect to God.
[2] Miebala: a god in heaven, who was in charge of the rainfall.

第三章 勐董板有七个姑娘

Canto 3 Seven Princesses in Mengdongban

离勐板加很远很远

在那云雾缥缈之间

有一个奇妙的地方

它的名字叫勐董板

勐董板是个好地方

遍地开鲜花

满山是牛羊

来往的人都骑着大象

勐董板的国王叫作"叭团"①

他有七个一般大小的姑娘

她们像七只飞雁

披上孔雀的羽毛

就能在天空飞翔

七个公主啊

七朵海棠

花中有花王

最鲜艳的花朵

要算喃婼娜——第七个姑娘

---

① 叭团:直译为魔鬼的头人,在此当"孔雀国王"解释。

Far away from Mengbanjia,

In the clouds and mist,

There was a wonderful place

Called Mengdongban[①].

Mengdongban was a nice place

With so many blooming flowers.

Cattle and sheep were all over the mountains and plains,

People rode on elephants to and fro.

The King of Mengdongban was known as Batuan,

The father of seven girls of similar figure.

The seven girls looked like seven flying geese.

When they put on their peacock feathers,

They could go flying in the sky.

Seven princesses

Were like seven Malus spectabilis,

There must be a queen among the flowers.

Here the most bright and beautiful one

Was Nanruona, the little princess.

---

① Mengdongban: The story began over nine thousand years ago. There were 101 states along the Lancang River. Mengdongban was the richest and the most beautiful state among them. People often called it Peacock Kingdom. −Translator's note

密密丛丛的树林里

有一个镜子般的金湖碧波荡漾

美丽的凤凰在那里栖息

多情的金鹿在望着水中的情郎

湖边有一座古寺

古寺里住着一个"叭拉纳西^①"

他像蜜蜂一样日夜念经

古寺里的钟声悠悠扬扬

每隔七天

七个美丽的姑娘飞到湖边

每隔七天

湖边的花都为她们开放

雀鸟悄悄飞来偷看

只见千万层白花花的水浪中

七朵鲜花一晃一晃

---

① 叭拉纳西，据说是佛教传入中国初期在森林中修行的和尚。

In the thick forest,

There was a mirror-like golden rippling lake

Where the beautiful phoenixes roosted.

An amorous golden deer was gazing at her lover in the water.

An old temple was right here by the lake,

A monk called Bala'naxi[1] practiced there,

He chanted scripture day and night, buzzing like bees.

The sound of temple bell reverberated in the forest.

Every seven days

The seven princesses came to the lakeside;

Every seven days

The flowers around the lake were blooming to welcome them.

Birds came to peep.

They saw seven flowers swaying their bodies

In millions of ripples, white and shining.

---

[1] Bala'naxi: In the legend, Bala'naxi was a monk who practised in the forest when Buddhism was first introduced into China.

第四章 猎人

Canto 4 The Hunter

从竹林中跑出一个猎人

骑着马拿着弩箭

他追逐着一只金鹿

从树林里追到湖边

他忽然站在岸旁

就像拴牛的木桩

金鹿从他脚上奔过

他也没有看见

想吃鱼的翡翠鸟总是蹲在水边

蝙蝠一看见佛寺就绕着飞转①

年轻的猎人啊

他的眼睛就像两颗明珠

沉落在湖水中间

落日把他的影子送到水面

惊动了七朵浮莲

好像麻雀看见了老鹰

她们披起羽毛飞向远方

湖水又恢复了平静

鸟雀也飞回森林

①"蝙蝠绕寺飞"是傣族成语。据传说从前有一个和尚,被头人赶出佛寺,无家可归,由于他怀念佛寺,后来变为一只蝙蝠绕着佛寺飞。

A hunter rushed out of the bamboo forest,

Riding on a horse with an arrow in his hand.

He was chasing a golden deer

From the forest down to the lakeside.

Suddenly he stood on the bank,

Like a wooden stake for a buffalo.

He did not even see

The golden deer run past him.

The hungry black-capped kingfisher always stood near the water.

On seeing a temple, a bat would circle around①.

O young hunter,

His eyes were like two shining pearls,

Shining in the middle of the lake.

Cast on the surface by the sunset,

His shadow frightened the seven floating lotuses.

Just like a sparrow seeing an eagle,

They put on their feathers and flew away.

The lake was calm again,

The birds were back in the forest.

---

① Once upon a time, there was a monk who was driven out of a temple, homeless. And then, as he missed the temple, he turned into a bat and circled around each temple.

只有猎人啊

还在呆呆望着青天

钟声突然把他惊醒

骏马呜呜嘶鸣

他揉一揉眼睛

便打马来到寺院

猎人跪在叭拉纳西的脚下

求他解开爱情的锁链

"都卓龙"① 啊

我不知道是在梦里

还是真正活在人间

"我看见湖里有七个姑娘

像莲花一样发出清香

金色的带子装饰在头上

脖子上的珠宝闪烁发光

"可是，她们已经飞向天堂

美丽的天使啊

像彩虹使我眼晕

像老鹰叼去了我的心脏"

———————————
① 都卓龙直译为大佛爷。

Only the poor hunter
Still looked up at the sky blankly.

He was abruptly awakened by the bell,
The steed neighed again and again.
Rubbing his eyes, he rode on the horse,
And went back to the temple.

The hunter kneeled down before Bala'naxi
And begged him to unlock the love chain.
"O Dubeilong[①]
I doubt whether I am lingering about in my dream
Or alive in the world."

"I saw seven beautiful girls swimming in the lake,
And smelt their lotus fragrance.
Their heads were decorated with golden ribbons,
Glittering jewelry encircled their necks."

"Yet they have flown to paradise.
O beautiful angels,
Like rainbows their beauty dazzled me,
Like eagles they have carried off my heart."

---

① Dubeilong was used to address a highly respected monk in temple.

叭拉纳西问他是哪里来的猎人
他说他是勐板加的小王子
刚生下来的时候
大家就叫他召树屯

叭拉纳西眯起了眼睛
冷冷地笑了一声
召树屯哀求道："请你不要笑我
我确确实实喜欢她们"

"青年人啊，你抬一抬头
这是佛寺，这是佛身
你还活在人间
就应该遵守人的本分

"她们是天王的公主
她们是神仙的化身
世间从来就没有一条路
通到那个地方

"丢了你的梦想
你不是'锦那丽'

Bala'naxi asked where the hunter came from,

He answered he was the little prince of Mengbanjia.

When he was born,

He was named Zhaoshutun.

Bala'naxi squinted his eyes,

And sneered at him.

Zhaoshutun implored, "Please do not laugh at me,

I really do love them."

"Poor young man, please raise your head.

This is a Buddhist temple and the Avalokitesvara figure.

As you are still living,

You should obey the rules of man."

"They are the princesses of heaven's emperor,

The incarnations of the Goddess.

There is no road in the world

Leading to that place."

"Give up your dream.

You are not Jinnali.

你也没有'锦那暖'① 的翅膀

就好像爬上树去捉鱼

就好像下到水里捞月亮"

猎人懊恼地拜别了叭拉纳西

像白天的猫头鹰飞出树林

他牵着马又来到金波荡漾的湖旁

用手轻轻拨起浪花

水波中又闪现出七朵红花

树影在水中晃动

七个姑娘对他微笑

慢慢朝他游浮

啊，那是红色的鱼在水中游弋

那是月亮和星星在湖中的光影

那是银河流向金湖

那是神龙带领着虾兵蟹将

在他的湖中巡行

神龙啊，你是我的好朋友

我曾经救过你的生命②

---

① 锦那丽、锦那暖，是两种飞得最快的鸟，传说每天飞绕大地七十七转。

② 传说召树屯在金湖边狩猎时看见一只老鹰将神龙叼入空中，召树屯用箭射死老鹰，救了神龙，后来他和神龙结为朋友。

Unlike Jinnanuan[①], you have no wings.

It's like catching a fish on a tree,

Or getting the moon in the water."

Disappointed, the hunter said goodbye to Bala'naxi.

Just like an owl flying out of the woods in the daytime.

He led a horse to the lake with golden ripples.

He paddled the water with his hand,

The seven red flowers flashed again in the waves.

The reflection of trees was swaying in the water.

These seven girls smiled at the hunter,

And swam towards him slowly.

Ah, they were red fish cruising freely.

They were the reflections of the moon and stars in the water,

They were the Milky Way flowing into the golden lake,

They were the shrimp soldiers and crab generals

Led by the Immortal Dragon, patrolling in his lake.

Dear Immortal Dragon, you are my good friend.

[①] Jinnali, Jinnanuan: In the legend, both Jinnali and Jinnanuan were the fastest birds in that place, and they circled around the earth 77 times each day.

如今我遇到困难
你能不能给我帮助

神龙浮出水面
张开嘴哈哈大笑
"我的朋友呀
什么风把你刮到这里"

"是病魔纠缠着你
还是有人来攻打勐板加
你是我的救命恩人
我一定为你效命"

猎人诉出了心中的苦恼
神龙又是一阵爽朗的大笑
接着就把七个姑娘的秘密
对召树屯讲了

Once I had saved your life①,

Now I am in trouble,

Would you like to give me a hand?

Coming to the surface,

The Immortal Dragon grinned with pleasure,

And said, "My dear friend,

What wind has blown you here?"

"Are you tortured by a disease

Or is your country attacked by an enemy?

You are my savior,

Undoubtedly I will work for you."

The hunter related his inner anguish.

The Immortal Dragon laughed loudly.

And then he told Zhaoshutun

All the secrets of the seven princesses.

---

① The story goes that when Zhaoshutun was hunting by the golden lake, he saw an eagle
snatch the Immortal Dragon and fly into the sky. Zhaoshutun shot down the eagle with
an arrow and saved the Dragon, who became his good friend.

第五章　告别

Canto 5　Farewell

召树屯按照神龙的话

用长刀砍了许多竹子

在大树上搭起了竹棚

他就躲在那里等候

过了一天又一天

月亮在湖里洗了七次脸

凤凰飞来饮了七次水

召树屯在湖边等了七天七夜

那一天无风无云

蓝空里飞来七只孔雀

她们轻轻地落在湖边

又像花一样飘落到水面

笑声泛起波纹

花朵飘向湖心

召树屯悄悄爬到湖岸

拿走了喃婼娜的孔雀衣

召树屯回到了竹棚

便放声歌唱

七个姑娘慌忙回到岸上

喃婼娜不见了衣裳

Following the instructions of the Immortal Dragon,

Zhaoshutun chopped down many bamboo trees

To build a bamboo shed

In a big tree where he hid and waited.

Day after day, at the same lake,

The moon washed its face seven times,

Phoenixes drank water seven times,

By the lake the prince waited seven days and seven nights.

On a clear and windless day,

Seven peacocks came from the blue sky,

They settled lightly on the lakeside

And then dropped to the surface of the lake like seven flowers.

Laughter dimpled the surface of the lake,

The seven flowers floated toward the center.

The prince crept to the lakeside,

And took away the Peacock Princess Nanruona's feather dress.

Coming back to the bamboo shed,

He began to sing aloud.

The seven girls went ashore in haste,

And found the feather dress of the little princess was gone.

没有翅膀的鸟不会飞

没有鱼鳍的鱼不会游水

没有衣裳的喃婼娜

无法向天空追她的姐妹

歌声越来越近

喃婼娜慌忙躲进花丛

喃婼娜的手啊

被谁轻轻的牵动

六只孔雀在空中徘徊

她们看见猎人拉住了妹妹

像有六支箭射进她们的心中

像有六把刀砍在她们的身上

十二只翅膀

一齐扑向猎人

六个姐姐的头

一齐冲向召树屯

情人不会吐掉嘴里的槟榔 ①

姑娘不会轻易拔下头上的金簪

① 傣族青年男女在互相恋爱时，常用槟榔来款待情人。傣族人认为吃了槟榔的人
不能变心。

A bird could not fly without wings,

A fish could not swim without fins,

Without her feathers, the little princess

Could not catch up to her sisters in the sky.

The singing was getting closer,

Nanruona hastily hid herself

Among the flowers.

Her hand was gently held by someone.

The six other peacocks were hovering overhead,

They saw their little sister held by the hunter,

They felt as if their hearts were shot by six arrows,

And their bodies were chopped up by six knives.

All of a sudden,

They dived down from the sky

With their twelve flapping wings,

Heading directly for the hunter.

A lover would not spit areca nut[①] out at will;

A girl would not casually take her hairpin off;

---

① It was an old tradition of the Dai people. When the young man and woman fell in love
with each other, they'd entertain his/her partner with this areca nut. They believed
that the lovers who ate areca nut would not change their minds, so they would have an
eternal love.

召树屯不愿放走心爱的喃婼娜
六个姐姐的眼泪
雨滴般洒在湖上

"再见啊，可怜的喃婼娜
我们向你告别了
要是以前我们做错了什么事
妹妹呵，请你原谅我们

"当我们飞下来的时候
我们总是把你围在中间
现在你竟被猎人捉去
这一切都是命中注定

"我们赶回去告诉爹妈
阿妈会很伤心
阿妈会请求阿爹
赶快派兵来救你"

喃婼娜的眼睛望着天空
眼泪遮住了姐姐们的身影
她低下头说不出话
只向姐姐们"合掌"①

―――――――
① "合掌"：傣族的一种礼节，表示对对方的尊敬和诚意。

Zhaoshutun was unwilling to let her go.

Their tears the six sisters were

Pouring out upon the lake.

"Farewell, Nanruona,

We have to say goodbye to you.

If we did something wrong,

Please forgive us, my dear sister."

"When we fly downwards,

We always fly around you and protect you.

Now you are captured by the hunter.

It is your destiny."

"We shall go back and tell our parents.

Mother will be grieved,

Father will give orders,

Soldiers will be sent to rescue you."

Nanruona looked up into the sky,

Her tears blurred her eyes.

Lowering her head unable to say anything.

She put her palms together[①].

_____

① It is a polite custom showing respect and good faith to others.

"从今以后

我们恐怕不能相见

请把我的话转告父母和头人

喃婼娜啊

永远想念他们"

"From now on,

I am afraid we cannot see each other.

Please tell our parents and the tribal chief,

I, Nanruona,

Will miss them forever."

第六章 爱情
Canto 6　Love

湖水一片平静
喃婼娜微微打战
就像风雨飘到她的身上
她不知道猎人将对她怎样

召树屯轻轻脱下自己的衣裳
把它披在喃婼娜的身上
然后他跪在姑娘的面前
嘴里又轻轻歌唱

"美丽的姑娘啊
我像一只粗野的狼
我像无礼的暴君
我的心啊，像金鹿一样善良

"请雪白的云朵给我作证
请微风表白我的心肠
粉团花啊
我只是一只平常的蜜蜂

"请你不要再用双手遮住脸
只求你轻轻看我一眼
我知道，只要你看我一眼
你就会看清我的心房"

The water recovered its peace,

Nanruona wondered what would happen.

Her body trembled slightly,

As if hit by a sudden storm.

Zhaoshutun took off his coat,

And draped it over her shoulders.

Kneeling before the young lady,

He began to sing gently.

"Oh, my fair lady,

I am as rough as a wolf,

And as rude as a tyrant,

But my heart is as kind as a golden deer."

"The white cloud can testify for me,

The breeze can convey my love.

Oh, pink flower,

I am just an ordinary bee."

"Please don't cover your face with your hands,

Just take a look at me.

I know if you do,

You will read my heart."

喃婼娜依然一声不响

就像含羞草被人触动

她的眼睛啊

像天上的星星闪烁

椰子树没有他英俊

十五的月亮比不上他的眼睛

哪里来的小伙子呀

菠萝的滋味

也比不上他的歌声

召树屯恨不得拔出长刀

掏出自己的心房

他不知道该用什么办法

才能表白他的爱恋与敬仰

"多兰嘎①啊

请你打开谷仓

请你把爱情的种子

播在姑娘的心上

"姑娘啊

_____

① 多兰嘎：傣族传说中的爱神。

Nanruona, mum as a mimosa,

Kept quiet unless touched.

Her eyes,

Bright as the twinkling stars in the sky.

He was even more handsome than a coconut palm,

His eyes were much brighter than the full moon.

Where did he come from?

His singing was sweeter

Than a pineapple.

Zhaoshutun didn't know in what way

He could express his love and admiration for her.

He would even cut out his heart

With his dagger to prove his true love.

"O Duolan'ga[①],

Please open your barn door,

And sow the seeds of love

In her heart."

"My Lady,

---

① Duolan'ga was the god of love in Dai legend.

我不是狐狸

不会吃小鸡

我不是老虎

不会伤害人

"我是勐板加的一只丑鸭

我是猎人的一枝秃箭

我是田野上能望的鹭鸶①

我的名字叫作召树屯"

喃婼娜听见这个名字

不觉吃了一惊

摩古拉曾经说过

她将嫁给一个勇敢善良的人

她的心里暗暗喜欢

恰恰遇到了心上的人

召树屯的眼睛没有离开过喃婼娜

召树屯的嘴没有停止歌声

在喃婼娜没有对他回答之前

他决心一辈子歌唱不停

---

① 相传，鹭鸶与孔雀恋爱，因孔雀飞进森林里，鹭鸶等待孔雀，脖子都望长了。

I am not a fox,

So I will not eat chickens;

I am not a tiger,

So I will not hurt humans."

"I am an ugly duck from Mengbanjia,

I am like a blunt arrow to a hunter,

I am a silly egret stretching my neck[1],

My name is Zhaoshutun."

As Nanruona heard his name,

She was amazed.

Mogula had predicted

That she would marry a brave and kind man.

She was delighted secretly

About finding the right man.

Zhaoshutun didn't take his eyes off her,

Nor stop singing songs.

He would not stop singing

Until Nanruona opened her mouth.

---

[1] It was said that an egret fell in love with a peacock, the latter flew into a forest, and the former was waiting for her return and stretched its neck longer.

"可爱的姑娘啊
请打开你的心扉
不管天崩地裂
鱼啊，只有在水里才能生存

"我只要每天看见你一眼
没有吃的我也心甘
请你这朵花开在我园里
让我变成浇花的水"

母鸡听见公鸡叫唤会扇开翅膀
召树屯的歌声
像一只蜜蜂落在喃婼娜的心上
她望着湖水
又羞又喜地低声歌唱

"热辣辣的太阳
会使鲜花枯萎
你过热的爱情啊
叫我的心跳荡

"一棵芭蕉只结一次果
懂得修剪花蕊的人啊
芭蕉果会愈结愈多

"Lovely girl,

Please open your heart,

No matter what will happen.

A fish cannot live without water."

"If I can take a look at you every day,

I will be happy even without food.

If you are a flower in my garden,

I will be the water nourishing you."

On hearing a rooster's crow, a hen would flap her wings.

The prince's singing was like a honeybee,

Falling on the girl's heart.

Watching the water, shyly and happily

She started to sing in a low voice.

 "The scorching sun

Makes the flower wither.

Your fervent love

Makes my heart beat wildly."

"A banana tree bears fruit one time.

If it is pruned by an old hand,

There will be a good harvest."

"一棵香瓜只抽一次藤

会种香瓜的人啊

一棵香瓜爬满瓜棚

"愿你像一棵椰子树

树高根深

我会天天坐在树下

觉得快活凉爽"

召树屯的两颊发烫

心里像煮开的水一样

他站起身

放声歌唱

"姑娘啊

你的歌声像湖里的清水

让我洗了一次澡

姑娘啊

只有现在，我才感到

我是一个骄傲的国王

"姑娘啊

你看见没有

"The vine of the muskmelon sprouts up only once.

If it is planted by an old hand, on a pergola

There will be a good harvest."

"I wish you are like a coconut tree,

Tall and having deep roots,

I would sit under the tree,

And enjoy the cool and joy."

Zhaoshutun flushed shyly,

And his heart was as excited as boiling water.

Then he stood up,

And sang aloud.

"Lovely girl,

Your singing, like clear water,

Cleans my body thoroughly."

"Lovely girl,

Right now, I feel

I am a proud king."

"Lovely girl,

Have you seen

湖边的花为我们开放

林中的鸟也为我们歌唱"

召树屯轻轻拉起喃婼娜

一对情侣沿着湖岸

像凤凰一样漫舞低唱

That the flowers by the lake are blooming for us?

That the birds in the woods are singing for us?"

Zhaoshutun took her hand gently.

They walked along the lakeshore,

Singing and dancing, much like two phoenixes.

第七章 拴线礼

Canto 7 The Rite of Tying a Thread *

---

* 拴线礼是傣族的一种仪式，在祝贺结婚或为新生婴儿免除灾难的时候，都举行拴线礼，通常是由年长的人将一根红线拴在被祝贺人的手上，表示吉祥。

Tying a thread is a traditional rite of the Dai people. The adults usually perform a rite to celebrate the wedding, or sometimes they do it for their newborn babies to avoid misfortune and evil. In general, the person who is given best wishes will have a red thread tied on his wrist by an esteemed elder, which means praying for good fortune.

走出重重的森林

眼前是一片平坦的坝子

落日赶着成群的牛羊

村寨在彩霞中闪亮

召树屯指着坝子说

"看啊，喃婼娜

这就是我们的家乡

这就是我们的勐板加地方"

喃婼娜朝着召树屯指的方向眺望

一千间房子镶着金边

一万根栋梁雕刻了龙身

墙上画满了花草和飞鸟

喘息的马儿

扬起了灰尘

穿过田野

他们来到了城边

一阵咚咚的鼓声

召来了许多百姓

他们是来看喃婼娜

他们是来迎接召树屯

Walking out of the thick forest,

They saw a flatland.

Herds of sheep and cows were driven at dusk,

The sunset cast a glow over the villages and farmland.

Zhaoshutun pointed at that flatland,

And said, "Look, Nanruona,

This is our hometown,

Welcome to our Mengbanjia."

Nanruona overlooked that place in the distance,

Where hundreds of houses were edged with golden lines,

Where thousands of pillars were carved with dragons,

Where there were paintings of flying birds and flowers on the wall.

Horses dashed up the road,

Raising the dust behind them.

Across the field,

They reached the edge of the city.

At the sound of a drum-roll,

The villagers had a happy gathering

To see the beautiful girl, Nanruona,

And welcomed their prince, Zhaoshutun.

人们都赞赏喃婼娜的美丽

"这是一朵正要开放的腊梅花

勐板加地方

找不出这样一个美女"

召树屯把喃婼娜带回家里

头人和百姓都在议论

赶快给他们"拴线"

有的人给喃婼娜准备金伞

有人去准备"喃菩他"圣水 ①

全勐的百姓都来庆贺

他们送来了蜡条 ②

送酒的人像一条河

村村寨寨都为他们赶猪赶羊 ③

宫殿里响起三声大炮

像脚鼓、铓锣 ④ 一起敲响

百姓像朝王的蜜蜂

唱着、跳着涌进皇宫

---

① "喃菩他"圣水是七种金属粉混起来的溶液，传说用来洗澡，可以得到吉祥。
② 蜡条：是用黄蜡做成的细条，可以点燃，象征吉祥。
③ 傣族中凡头人土司结婚时，老百姓要送猪羊。
④ 铓锣：云南少数民族的一种打击乐器。——译者注

They all praised her beauty,

"This is a winter-sweet flower beginning to blossom.

She is the most beautiful girl

That we have ever seen."

Zhaoshutun brought her home,

The tribal chief and other villagers talked about

Performing the rite of tying the thread.

Someone was preparing a golden umbrella;

Someone was preparing Nanputa[①].

The villagers gathered there to celebrate,

They brought wax strips[②],

And continuously served wine.

The people from different villages drove sheep and pigs.[③]

Three guns thundered out a salute,

Like the sound of footed drums and gongs[④]

The crowd adored and worshipped their king like bees,

Swarming into the palace, dancing and singing.

---

① Nanputa, a kind of holy water in the legend, was a mixture of seven metal powders. It was said that if a man took a bath in it, he would have good fortune.

② Wax strip, made of wax, could be lit up to mark an auspicious omen.

③ In the tradition, when the tribal chiefs got married, the ordinary people had to offer sheep and pigs.

④ The gong is a percussion instrument in Yunnan. −Translator's note

一群侍女捧着蜡条跟着喃婼娜

来到大厅里，便一个个跪下

召树屯燃起蜡条走到她的身边

年老的阿爹手上拿了一根红线

轻轻地拴在他们的手上

又把蜡条吹熄

阿妈把他们扶到门边

大象把前腿跪在他们面前

召树屯和喃婼娜骑上大象

绕着村寨游了一圈

沿路都是百姓

跪在地上为他们滴水 ①

嘴里为他们祝福

孩子们都喊着"水！水！水！" ②

转眼就到了七月

许多果树都开花了

喃婼娜和召树屯

开始收割他们的爱情

---

① 滴水：用水滴在地上，是一种祝福的仪式。

② "水！水！水！"是欢呼声。

A group of maids followed Nanruona

With wax strips in their hands,

They walked into the hall and knelt down.

Zhaoshutun lit up a strip and came to her side,

An esteemed elder held a red thread,

And tied it on their wrists and then blew the strip out.

An old woman held their hands and led them to the door,

An elephant bent her forelegs and knelt before them.

The new couple mounted,

And started a parade around the villages.

There were many people clustering along the road,

They knelt down and dripped water[①]onto the ground.

Adults were blessing them,

Children shouted, "Shui! Shui! Shui!"[②]

Soon it was July

Many fruit trees were blossoming,

Zhaoshutun and Nanruona

Started to reap the fruit of their love.

---

① Dripping water is a traditional rite of sending best wishes by dripping water on the ground.

② "Shui!" is the Dai people's way of expressing excitement and joy. Here they are cheering for the new couple.

第八章　战争

Canto 8　The War

六个姐姐啊
像带箭的鸟儿飞回到勐董板
跌跌爬爬来到爹妈面前
她们哭泣得说不成声
把爹妈吓得心神不定

"爹妈啊
喃婼娜遭到了不幸
猎人把她捉去
如今生死不明"

突然来的雷鸣
叫人胆破心惊
突然来的消息
害得老妈妈昏迷不醒

六个女儿救起了老母亲
千万支箭射中了叭团的心
他一声不响
眼泪淌得泉水一样不停

喃婼娜是他们最小的姑娘
喃婼娜是他们掌上的明珠
喃婼娜是他们的心肝

The six sisters were like birds

With arrows in their bodies.

Sadly, they flew back to Mengdongban, to their parents.

They sobbed and were almost choked up,

Which upset their parents.

"O, my dear father and mother,

Nanruona suffered misfortune.

She was captured by the hunter.

We don't know whether she is still alive or not."

The sudden noise of thunder

Was frightening.

The unexpected news

Sent their mother into a coma.

Six daughters lifted her up.

Father kept silent all along,

As if his heart was shot by millions of arrows.

His tears were streaming down like the spring water.

Nanruona was the youngest,

She was as precious as a pearl,

She was their sweetheart,

喃婼娜从来没有离开过他们

喃婼娜的撒娇叫爹妈喜欢

喃婼娜的声音叫爹妈温暖

喃婼娜是家里的一只小鸟

只要她在家，人人都会快活

老妈妈从昏死中苏醒

她的眼泪哗哗流下

她的心像被撕成几片

她的声音像一根弦的"玎"①

"可怜的喃婼娜啊

不幸的姑娘

你在那里受难

哪个能够救你回家

"晚上有哪个给你铺床

哪个来代你睡在我的身旁

你啊，怎么忍心丢下阿妈

叫我怎样活下去……"

---

① 玎是傣族的一种乐器，类似二胡。傣族青年男女常常用玎传达感情。

She had never separated from them before.

Her parents were delighted by her childlike actions.

Her voice made them warm and happy,

She was a little bird in the family,

When she was at home, everyone was cheerful.

Mother came back to herself from the coma,

Her tears flowing without stop.

Her heart was torn into pieces.

She wept like the ding[①] instrument.

"Poor Nanruona,

How miserable you are,

You are suffering there,

Who can save you and take you home?"

"Who makes a bed for you at night?

Who sleeps by my side if not you?

How can you leave me alone?

How do I live without you?"

[①] The ding is a single-string instrument which is similar to the erhu. The young people of
the Dai ethnic group often play it to express their affection.

母亲再也哭不出声

叭团猛地站起身

他击起大鼓

下令立刻出兵

在勐板加地方

召树屯和喃婼娜正过着好时光

铓锣和大鼓突然齐响

竹楼都被震得摇晃

灾难来到了勐板加

勐板加人心惶惶

召树屯传下命令

勇敢的人都挂上刀枪

骑马的来到召树屯面前

骑象的集中在广场

他们摩拳擦掌

人啊，像被暴风吹打的树林一样

召树屯穿上全副盔甲

默默来到妻子面前

向喃婼娜轻轻告别

"亲爱的喃婼娜

Mother stopped crying now,

Batuan stood up suddenly,

He beat the drum,

And gave orders to his soldiers.

In Mengbanjia, the new couple

Were having a pleasant time.

Suddenly, gongs and drums were beaten loudly,

The bamboo sheds were shaken violently.

A disaster was at hand,

People got really scared,

Zhaoshutun commanded

That the warriors take up their weapons and get prepared.

Horse riders came to the prince,

Elephant riders gathered in the square.

They were well-prepared and ready for a fight.

People were like the trees just beaten by a windstorm.

Zhaoshutun, fully armed,

Walked to his wife quietly,

And said farewell to her,

"My sweetheart, I'm very sorry.

我们的日子刚开始
就遇到了不幸
不过，请你放心
我一定不会让你受惊

"大树倒了会惊散鸟群
灾难会伤害人的生命
我啊，不能不离开心爱的人
但是，我的心将永远在你身边

"我知道
没有弦的玎
弹不出声音
看不见的雷声
却总是跟着闪电"

好梦常被风雨惊醒，
喃婼娜的心里闪着霹雳
两股泪水淌过脸上
她低声对着丈夫唱吟

"你的爱情像血液一样
永远激荡着我的心房
在你的面前

We just got married,

But misfortune has befallen us.

Nevertheless, don't worry.

I will keep you safe."

"A falling tree will scatter a flock of birds,

A disaster will destroy human life.

I have to leave my beloved.

But my heart will be with you forever."

"I know,

Without its string

A Ding cannot make a sound,

The hidden thunder

Always comes after the lighting."

A sweet dream is often broken up by the rainstorm.

Tears ran down her cheeks.

As if there was a thunderbolt in her heart,

She lowered her voice and chanted,

"Your love is like the blood,

Always surging in my heart.

You make me warm,

就像在冬天的火塘旁

"请你不要为我伤心
请你不要为我怕去打仗
你的妻子
一万年都是为你活着

"你要很好地带领那些勇士
不要让他们斜着眼睛看你
他们都是正直的人
他们会帮助你杀退仇敌

"我在家里
会用最真诚的心
祈求神灵帮助你
你会感觉到
你的妻子随时都站在你身旁

"去啊，不要说时间长
椰子要十年才会结果
葵花总是向着太阳
你一定会得胜
欢乐的日子会像青松一样"

Like sitting by a burning stove in winter."

"Please don't worry about me,

Please don't shrink back in battle.

For your wife

Will live for many years waiting for you."

"Lead these warriors to the battlefield.

Don't let them look down upon you.

All of them are men of integrity,

They will help you defeat the enemy."

"I will stay at home,

And sincerely pray,

Pray to God

For help, you will feel

Your wife is always by your side."

"Just go, it will not take a long time.

A coconut tree needs ten years to bear fruit,

Sunflowers are always growing towards the sun.

You will win a victory someday.

Our happy life will be as long as the pine tree."

喃婼娜说完话
又亲了亲他的头巾
召树屯便走出城门
大象已经来到他面前

他带领着八万人马
浩浩荡荡绕过田坝
穿过密密的森林
向边界出发

With these words,

Nanruona kissed his turban again.

Zhaoshutun walked out of the gate,

The elephant was already there waiting for him.

He led eighty thousand troops

Heading to the border,

Along the way they bypassed fields,

And walked through forests.

第九章 灾难

Canto 9　The Disaster

召树屯离开了家乡

灾难就落在喃婼娜身上

有一个晚上

召树屯的阿爹做了一个梦

梦见他的肠子从肚子里飞出

绕着城池转了三转

他坐着肠子

像乘着飞龙在上空游转

然后肠子又回到他的身上

他被怪梦惊醒

一直呆坐到天亮

是凶是吉

叫他十分忐忑不安

他把所有的摩古拉都请来

那个最大的摩古拉掐指一算

脸色就发白

话到舌尖又吞了回去

什么事情使摩古拉作难

什么事情叫摩古拉不敢抬头

Soon after the prince left his hometown,

A disaster befell Nanruona.

One night,

The King had a dream

Where his intestines flew out of his belly,

Circling three times around the city.

He rode on them, flying in the sky.

As if he roamed freely on a flying dragon,

And then his intestines flew back into his belly again.

He was awakened by the strange dream,

Staring blankly till daybreak.

What did it mean?

He felt upset about the omen.

So he sent for all Mogula.

When the grand Mogula did the divinations for the King,

He looked pale after finishing them.

He dared not speak out the truth.

What did he worry about?

Why did he lower his head?

经过国王再三请求
摩古拉才说出口

"灾难就要像火一样燃烧
只因为你家里有了妖气
一棵树结不出两种果子
喃婼娜生得再漂亮
也不能和人住在一起"

国王愕然抬起头
半信半疑地望着摩古拉
他要摩古拉再三推算

摩古拉把头低下
装作诚心诚意
掐着指头算了又算
他皱起眉毛眯起了眼睛
嘴里吐出了骇人的字眼

"只有杀了喃婼娜
用她的血来祭百姓的神
才能消除百姓的灾难
才能叫你重生"

The King repeatedly urged,

He was reluctant to tell the truth.

"Disaster is like fire, burning and spreading.

The reason is that there is an evil in the palace.

As we know, a fruit tree cannot bear two types of fruit.

Although Nanruona is very pretty,

She cannot live with humans."

The King raised his head in astonishment,

Stared at Mogula skeptically,

And asked him to divine it once again.

Mogula lowered his head in astonishment,

And pretended to be honest and serious,

Counting it on his fingers again and again.

Then, scowling and squinting,

He spoke out some terrifying words.

"All we can do is to kill Nanruona,

Her blood will be sacrificed to the gods.

The disaster can be eliminated,

And you will be reborn."

国王想了又想
既然是妖气就要除根
他问摩古拉
她该死在什么时辰

摩古拉烧起香火
庄严地宣布
"她将死在龙日
太阳刚刚上升的时刻"

时刻到了
乌云像青纱盖住太阳
勐板加一片阴暗、凄凉
百姓围在宫殿门前
眼睛都黯然无光

喃婼娜被叫唤出来
她脸上绯红，满怀高兴
以为百姓聚集门前
是来迎接丈夫得胜回转

当国王向她述说真情
就像魔鬼撕碎了她的心
她几次昏倒又几次苏醒

The King thought it over,

And finally made a resolution to kill her.

He asked Mogula about the best time

When they should end her life.

After burning the incense,

Mogula declared in a solemn manner,

"She will be put to death at the moment of daybreak

On the Day of the Dragon."

The time for the execution was coming,

Dark clouds, like a green curtain, blocked out the sun.

This place was shrouded in gloominess and dreariness,

People swarmed around the palace gate,

Their eyes dim and gloomy.

Nanruona was called out,

Her face blushing with happiness.

She thought people would gather here

To welcome her husband on his triumphant return.

When the King told her the truth, she was hurt

As if her heart was torn into pieces by the devil.

She fainted and awakened again and again,

跪在国王的面前哀哀求情

"阿爹啊

我本来是天上的一只神鸟

因为和你的儿子有缘

才从天上飞来

"我不会给你们带来灾难

求你不要听信谗言

只有阿爹的保护

暗箭才射不中我的身

"请你为你尊贵的儿子想一想

当他得胜回来

看不见心爱的妻子

他的心将会碎裂

"阿爹啊

没有水的树不会发芽

没有伴的雁啊

会伤心而死"

国王不敢抬眼去看喃婼娜

他只说:"不杀你

She knelt down and implored the King.

"Dear father,
I am an immortal bird in heaven.
It is destiny that let me come down to earth,
And marry your son."

"I will never bring disaster to you.
Please don't believe the slander.
I can't survive without your protection,
As hidden arrows are hard to guard against."

"Please think about your son,
When he returns and learns
That his wife is missing,
He will be heartbroken.

"Dear father,
A tree will not sprout without water.
A wild goose will die of sadness,
If his mate is gone."

The King dared not look up at her.
He said, "If I don't kill you,

勐板加就会遭难
召树屯也不能回转"

喃婼娜脸色苍黄
她的心像风中的布旗一样飘荡
她又向百姓求情
百姓都低头无声

喃婼娜十分伤心
脸上流下两行眼泪
她把头低下
等待死的时辰

死的时刻已将来临
她对阿妈告别
她说："阿妈啊
我的命运既然是这样
我也只有听从

"召树屯回来的时候
请你为我向他告别
倒了的松树还有根
枯了的青草还会再生"

People will suffer misfortune,

My son may not return."

Nanruona looked pale,

Her heart flaunting like a banner in the wind.

Then she asked the people for help.

But they bowed their heads and kept silent.

She looked very sad,

Tears running down her face.

She lowered her head,

And quietly waited for death.

It was time for the execution,

She said farewell to the Queen,

"My mother,

If it is doomed,

I can only accept it."

"When my husband is back,

Please send my farewell to him.

The fallen pine still has roots,

The withered grass will regrow."

阿妈洒下了伤心泪
走上前去轻轻抚摸喃婼娜的头发
问喃婼娜还有什么话说

喃婼娜擦干了眼泪
她说："我是从舞蹈的地方飞来
当我临死的时刻
我只有一个请求

"请求把我的羽毛还给我
让我最后跳一次舞
再享一次人生的欢乐
我会安心地离开人世"

国王看了一看百姓
所有的眼睛都好像说
"人就要死了
国王应该答应"

阿妈怯生生地抱出了孔雀衣
喃婼娜接过来穿在身上
她拜了拜阿妈
就轻轻起舞

With tears on her cheeks, the Queen

Came up to Nanruona, gently stroked her hair,

And asked if she had anything else to say."

Nanruona wiped her tears

And said, "I come from a place

Where people love to dance,

So I have a request at the last moment.

"Please give my feathers back to me,

Please let me dance for the last time

And enjoy the happy moment.

Then I will leave quietly."

The King glanced at the crowd,

It seems as if their eyes spoke,

"She is going to die,

Please fulfill her dream."

The Queen held the feathers in fear.

Nanruona put it on,

And bowed to the Queen.

Then she danced gracefully.

她抬起头向四面张望

四面都围满了百姓

看过一个一个脸孔

就是不见召树屯

她向百姓拜别

然后飞向屋顶

当她的脚离开了土地

眼泪像点点细雨

"阿爹阿妈啊，再见

头人们啊，再见

百姓们啊，再见

勐板加啊，再见

"愿你们都过好日子

愿你们万寿无疆

愿勐板加地方啊

五谷丰收，遍地牛羊

"再见啊，我住过的房屋

再见啊，我走过的小路

再见啊，亲爱的城市

再见啊，召树屯的家乡

She raised her head and looked around.
There were so many people around her.
She examined their faces one after another,
Not finding her husband.

She bid farewell to the ordinary people,
And then flew towards the roofs.
Her tears were falling like raindrops
When her feet left the earth.

"Farewell, my dear father and mother!
Farewell, tribal chiefs!
Farewell, my dear people!
Farewell, Mengbanjia!"

"I wish you a happy life!
I wish you a long life!
I wish this place will be prosperous and flourishing,
Full of crops and cattle.

"Farewell, my old house!
Farewell, the path I have traveled!
Farewell, my dear city!
Farewell, Zhaoshutun's hometown!

"请将我的话转告主人
我就要飞回勐董板
要是他怀念我的时候
就找一找别的姑娘吧

"千万请他把我忘记
我是一只无情的鸟
我就要飞回勐董板
勐董板是在另一个世界"

喃婼娜展开翅膀
她穿过云层飞向远方
不久，她又飞转回来
在勐板加上空盘旋

她又向勐板加告别
但是她的头依旧不断回转
仿佛她掉落了东西
仿佛她忘记了金簪

喃婼娜飞来飞去
又停在一棵黄金果树上
森林里所有的鸟都飞来朝拜

"Please pass my words to your lord,

I will go back to Mengdongban.

If he misses me,

He can find another girl instead.

"Let him forget me,

I am a heartless bird,

I have to go back to Mengdongban,

Which is in another world."

She spread her wings,

Flying away through clouds.

Soon she turned back,

And circled over the old place.

Once again she bid farewell to Mengbanjia,

But she turned around again and again,

As if she forgot something,

As if she had left her golden clasp.

Nanruona flew back and forth,

Resting on a golden fruit tree.

The birds in the forest came to pay respect to her,

她又渴又累，昏昏欲睡

鸟儿在四面歌唱
喃婼娜一惊
好像看见召树屯
啊，不，这是召树屯在怀念……

她匆匆飞起
又飞回到金湖边
最初的爱恋
又涌现在她眼前

她再没有力量远飞
两眼只是呆呆地望着湖水
夜雾的冷气把她惊醒
她才慢慢走到佛寺

她拜见了叭拉纳西
要求借宿一夜
叭拉纳西问她从哪里来
是不是从天上来到人间

"我不是出来游玩
我的丈夫是召树屯

She was exhausted, thirsty and sleepy.

Birds were singing around her,

She was startled,

As if she had seen her husband.

Ah, no, it was Zhaoshutun thinking of her…

She flew up in a hurry.

And went back to the lakeside

Where they met and fell in love.

The past scene rose before her eyes.

She had no strength to fly farther,

Just staring at the water blankly.

By night awakened by the cold fog,

She walked slowly to the temple.

She paid a visit to Bala'naxi,

And asked for lodging overnight.

Bala'naxi asked

If she came from paradise.

"I am not having a trip,

I come here for my husband.

只因为他去打仗
灾难降落到我的身上

"如果我的丈夫来到
请你劝他不要去寻找
前面没有人走的道路
野兽到处都会吃人

"请把这个金手镯转给他
要是他怀念我
请他问一问金手镯"

第二天一早
喃婼娜又从佛寺飞起
穿过森林和云彩
飞回自己的家乡

Because he went to battle,

A disaster fell upon me."

"If my husband comes to look for me,

Please persuade him not to do it.

There is no road for human beings ahead.

Wild beasts will eat him if he goes on."

"This is my bracelet,

Please give it to him.

If he misses me, he can ask it for my whereabouts."

The next morning,

Nanruona flew off from the temple.

Through the clouds and forests,

She was back in her hometown.

第十章 追赶

Canto 10　The Chase

战争已经胜利结束
勐板加的百姓热热闹闹
吹起金号银号
迎接自己的亲人

召树屯在人群中
找寻自己的妻子
喃婼娜啊
为什么不见你出来欢迎

为什么看不见妻子的面
听不见喃婼娜的声音
他急忙向房里走去
像有什么蒙住了心

他在房门前大喊
"我的喃婼娜呀
你还不曾起床
还是有了什么疾病

"你是躲在房里绣花
还是忙着梳妆打扮
难道是金花没有戴好
头发还没有梳完"

The war was over.

People heard the good news,

They tooted their horns to welcome

The warriors on their triumphant return.

In the crowd,

Zhaoshutun was looking for his wife,

"My darling, where are you?

Why not come out to see me?"

Yet he couldn't see her face,

Or even hear her voice.

He ran into the house,

Feeling very upset.

He shouted at the doorway,

"My dear Nanruona,

Haven't you gotten up yet?

What happened? Are you sick?"

"Are you doing your needlework?

Or dressing up?

Aren't you wearing your golden flower?

Haven't you finished doing your hair yet?"

头人们向他深深告罪
吃吃地把详情说出
最后，又把喃婼娜的话
小心地转告给他

召树屯呆了半天
像一只飞在空中的鸟
遭到猎人的暗箭
突然跌落下来

什么话也说不出
眼泪像小河一样流淌
他拜见父母
像一块石头落在地上

许久许久没有听见声音
阿爹阿妈都着了急
他们把召树屯扶起
故意问他为什么这样伤心

"阿爹啊阿妈
我虽然活着回来
我的心已经破碎

Tribal chiefs asked him for forgiveness,

And stammered out the whole story in detail.

Cautiously they passed him the words

Which Nanruona left.

Zhaoshutun was stunned,

Just like a bird,

Shot by a hidden arrow,

Falling out of the sky.

He couldn't speak a word,

His tears running like a river.

To his parents he kneeled,

As if a stone fell to the ground.

For a good while he didn't make a sound,

His parents worried,

They helped him up,

And asked him the reason on purpose.

"My dear father and mother,

Though I have come back alive,

My heart is broken."

"请允许我
去找寻可怜的喃婼娜
她住的地方对别人是太远
对我来说，只在眼前"

阿爹阿妈听见儿子的话
心里像一团乱麻
刚出山的太阳
又被乌云遮住
刚回家的儿子
又要离开爹妈

"我尊贵的英雄呀
听一听你父亲的话

"各勐都有好姑娘
我要出一道布告
把所有的姑娘都召来
任由你挑选"

召树屯立刻回答
"几千几万的姑娘都漂亮
她们统统都是好姑娘

"Please allow me

To look for my poor Nanruona.

She lives far away, but in my eyes,

She is right here by my side."

After hearing what he said,

His parents were extremely upset.

As if the rising sun was blocked

By the dark clouds again,

Their son, who had just come back home,

Would leave once again.

"My honorable hero,

Please follow your father's will.

"Nice girls can be found everywhere.

Once the decree is proclaimed,

All girls will be brought here.

You can choose anyone you like."

Zhaoshutun replied at once,

"All of them are

Beautiful and nice,

却没有一个活在我心上

"只要我还有一口气
我就会去找寻喃婼娜"
召树屯带上吃食和弓箭
立刻出门寻找爱人

他又来到金湖边
闻到"洛金坎"① 的芳香
怎么能叫他对妻子不怀想
他又坐在湖边低声哭唱

"喃婼娜啊
难道我将死在这里
喃婼娜啊喃婼娜
难道我们再也不能相见"

他又来到佛寺
拜见了叭拉纳西
叭拉纳西对他早已熟悉
他便眯起眼睛

---

① 洛金坎是一种黄色味香的野花，常常寄生于古树上。

But no one can live in my heart."

"As long as I can breathe,

I will find Nanruona."

Then he took food and arrows with him,

And started on his journey to find his wife.

Back at the Golden Lake,

Enjoying the fragrance of luojinkan,[①]

He missed his wife deeply.

Then he sat by the lake, singing and crying.

"Nanruona, my dear,

Shall I die here?

Nanruona, my dear,

May I see you again?"

He came to the temple,

And visited Bala'naxi

Who knew him well.

The monk narrowed his eyes.

---

① Luojinkan is the name of a wild flower, yellow and with a fragrant aroma, a parasitic plant which grows on old trees.

"你是个有福的人

你熟读了许多佛经

我走得十分疲倦

请你让我歇息一夜

"你问我为什么来

我是一个过路人

我是失掉鞘的剑

我是找寻妻子的人

"喃婼娜是不是经过这里

我应该怎样去找寻

善良的人啊

请你给我指点"

叭拉纳西站在他面前

说话好像念经

"曾经有朵云彩飘过金湖

曾经有一只孔雀飞过天空

"她有一颗纯洁的心

给你留下一只手镯

她劝你另娶妻了

她劝你把她忘记"

"You are a lucky man,

As you read many scriptures.

I am exhausted now.

May I stay for a night?"

"I came here for a reason.

I pass by here,

Looking for my wife.

I am a sword without a sheath."

"Nanruona must have been here before.

How can I find her?

You are so kind,

Please tell me."

Bala'naxi stood before him,

Like chanting scriptures, he said,

"There was a cloud floating over the Golden Lake;

There was a peacock flying over the sky."

"She has a pure heart,

She has left you a gold bracelet

And a message that you can marry another girl

And then forget her."

召树屯接过了金手镯

好像托着喃婼娜

心里像火烧一样难过

泪水又不禁流淌

行商的人结伴同行

马铃响得咚咚叮叮

出门的人成双成对

为什么只有他独自一人

"都卑龙啊

你有一颗慈善的心

请你告诉我

我应该怎样去找寻"

叭拉纳西低沉的声音

使召树屯心里难过

他说："你好好地听着

我要依照喃婼娜的话对你劝告

"那里有滚腾的风沙

那里的山有几万丈高

飞鸟过不去

Zhaoshutun took the gold bracelet

As if he held his wife.

His heart was like a burning fire,

Tears running like a river.

A group of merchants came along,

The horse bells were jingling all the way.

People came in pairs to the street.

It was Zhaoshutun who stayed alone.

"O Dubeilong,

You are kind-hearted,

Please tell me

How I can find her."

Bala'naxi spoke in a lower voice

Which made Zhaoshutun feel sad,

"Please listen carefully,

Nanruona has given you some advice."

"There is strong wind and rolling sand.

There are steep mountains

That no birds can fly over,

野兽走不通

"我没有什么法术

也没有什么口诀

我劝你转回头

勐板加还有许多姑娘

勐董板不是你去的地方"

召树屯再三请求

"所有的姑娘头髻都偏朝一边 ①

所有的姑娘和我都没有姻缘

请你把喃婼娜的话说完

我相信：她还给我留下一颗心"

叭拉纳西感到十分为难

他说他是念经的人

他只能祈求帕召 ②

为人们消灾免难

召树屯辞别了叭拉纳西

他又回到湖边

双手捧起了湖水

---

① 傣族姑娘喜欢把发髻梳朝一边，在傣族成语中有"不合心意"之意。
② 傣族称佛为"帕召"。

And no beasts can get through."

"I am not a magician,

And I don't know incantation.

You'd better go home

Where good girls are innumerable.

Mengdongban is not the right place."

Zhaoshutun repeated his request,

"All the girls wear a bun to one side[①],

Which means I'm not to their liking.

Please tell me what Nanruona said.

I believe she has left her pure heart."

Bala'naxi felt embarrassed.

He said he was a monk,

So he could only pray to Pa Zhao[②]

To avoid disaster and misfortune.

Zhaoshutun said farewell to him,

And went back to the lakeside,

Holding water with his hands, waiting and watching.

---

① In the Dai culture, if a girl keeps her bun to one side, it means something or someone is not to her taste.

② The Dai people address Buddha as Pa Zhao.

神龙的笑声卷起了波浪
它问召树屯又遇到什么困难

召树屯回答
"我的妻子离开了我
我要去把她寻找
她住在勐董板地方
鸟雀也飞不到她的家乡

"神龙啊，树木不能离开土地
月亮哪能离开太阳
我离开了喃婼娜
像葫芦离开了葫芦秧"

神龙十分同情召树屯
慷慨地给了他两种灵药一枝神箭
第一种药能够起死回生
第二种药能够解除疲倦
神箭可以打破一切阻拦

召树屯十分感激
他向神龙拜了三拜
作了九个揖
便又匆匆起程

The laughter of the Immortal Dragon made waves.

He asked Zhaoshutun what had happened.

Zhaoshutun replied,

"My wife left me.

I'm going to find her.

She lives in Mengdongban

Where even the birds cannot go."

"My friend, trees can not grow without the earth,

The moon can not exist without the sun.

So I cannot live without Nanruona,

No more than a calabash without its seedling."

The Dragon expressed sympathy to him,

And gave him two elixirs and an arrow.

One elixir can resurrect the dead,

The other can relieve tiredness.

The arrow can clear away any barriers.

Zhaoshutun felt thankful,

So he knelt down to the Dragon three times.

And bowed nine times,

Then set out again in a hurry.

他走了三百三十三天
不知走过多少森林高山
野兽不来伤害他
妖魔不敢靠近他的身边

晚上他就睡在大树下
猫头鹰飞来和他做伴
他比太阳先起床
他比金鹿先出森林

这一天
他走到一条河边
河水像一条黑布
蜿蜒在森林中间

召树屯抽出宝剑
插进水中
剑尖就被熔化
从此，他的宝剑就没有了剑尖

他向四处张望
对着河水叹息
　"难道就是这条河啊

After three hundred and thirty-three days,

He went through countless forests and mountains.

The beasts did not dare to harm him,

Neither did any evil.

By night he slept under a big tree,

Accompanied by an owl.

He got up before sunrise;

He stepped out of the forest earlier than the golden deer.

One day,

He came to a river bank.

The water was like a black cloth,

Coiling through the forests.

Zhaoshutun drew his sword,

And stuck it into the water.

The point was melted.

Hence, his sword had no point.

He looked around

And sighed deeply,

"Is it the river that will get in my way

拦住我走到妻子面前"

他沿着河边徘徊
一条巨蟒横在河面
他把神龙的药搽在脚底
飞一样踏上蟒身走过河去

召树屯又走了三百三十三天
前面出现了三座奇怪的石山
三座石山互相摩擦撞击
像风车一样旋转

想从天上飞过
可惜没有翅膀
想从地下穿过
地又没有洞穴

路啊，不能被阻拦
他拿起那枝神箭
唆的射向石山
哗啦一声
石块飞向两边

When I look for my wife?"

He wandered along the river.

A python blocked his way.

Spreading the elixir on his feet,

He jumped onto the python and crossed the river.

Zhaoshutun walked for another three hundred and thirty-

    three days,

Before him there were three weird stone mountains.

They were grinding and clashing,

Rotating like windmills.

Without wings

He couldn't fly over the mountain.

Without a tunnel

He couldn't go through the stone.

Nothing could block the way.

He held up the magic arrow,

And shot it into the mountains.

With a big noise,

Broken stones flew in opposite directions.

随着空中的黄尘

召树屯穿过石山

回头一看

石块又合成三座石山

又走了三百三十三天

召树屯来到砂石的海洋旁边

只见一片烟雾

下面的砂石沸腾滚卷

召树屯站在一棵大树下

只听见大风呼呼响

眼睛无法睁开

"喃婼娜啊

难道我就这样被阻拦

我们再也不能见面

难道没有一种方法

让我走到你的身边"

召树屯坐了下来

猜想着砂石的海洋有多宽

猜想着海洋底下有没有鱼龙

什么东西能够帮助他渡到对岸

In the dust,

Zhaoshutun went through the mountains.

Looking back, he saw that

The three mountains had recovered their normal shape.

After another three hundred and thirty-three days,

Zhaoshutun arrived at a sea

Where the beach was full of gravel and smoke,

The lower gravel was rolling and roaring.

Zhaoshutun stood under a big tree.

The wind was so strong

That he couldn't open his eyes.

"Nanruona, does it mean

I will be stopped here?

I can't see you again?

I must find a way

To come to your side again."

Zhaoshutun sat down, thinking about

How vast the gravel ocean was,

Whether there were any dragons or not,

How to cross and reach the other side.

他羡慕一阵阵刮过的大风
他羡慕天空中飘过去的白云
"白云呀，请告诉喃婼娜吧
要是我不能过去
就让我死在这里

"我死了也会化为一阵风
要是她的门是朝北边开
我就会吹进她的屋里
要不然我会变为一朵白云
飘到她的屋顶

"早上我看她梳妆
白天我听她歌唱
晚上啊，我会感觉到
她对我的怀想"

天色晚了
鹈托朗开始啼唱
召树屯觉得全身酸痛
他昏昏睡在树下

半夜里

He admired the gale and the white clouds,

Since he couldn't travel at will.

"White clouds, please pass my words to Nanruona

That if I cannot cross the ocean,

Let me die here."

"I would turn into a gust of wind,

If her door opens to the north,

I would get into her room,

Or I would turn into a white cloud,

Floating over her roof."

"In the morning, I can see her dressing.

In the daytime, I can hear her singing.

In the evening, I can feel

Her yearning."

It was getting dark.

The night bird began to sing.

Zhaoshutun felt pain from head to toe.

He slept deeply under the tree.

In the middle of the night,

他被什么声音惊醒

睁眼一看

一对"婼哈里林"^①站在树上

雌鸟十分忧愁

她说："如今生活难讨

明天又到哪里去找寻食物"

雄鸟回答："你不必担忧

勐董板的喃婼娜回到了家

叭团要杀象为她庆贺"

召树屯暗暗喜欢

他像蚂蚁一样爬到树上

躲在雌鸟翅膀下

用宝剑挖开了毛管

就钻到里边躲藏

不久就听见马鹿鸣叫

大雾降落下来

天色渐渐发亮

两只大鸟扇起了翅膀

飞到海洋中间

---

① 婼哈里林：傣族传说是一种最大的鸟。

He was awakened by a sound,

And opened his eyes.

He saw a pair of ruohalilin birds[①] sitting on the tree.

The female bird was depressed.

She asked, "Nowadays, our life is tough.

So where can we find our food?"

The male bird replied, "Don't worry,

Nanruona has returned.

Batuan will kill an elephant to celebrate."

Zhaoshutun was secretly pleased.

He climbed up the tree like an ant,

Hiding under the wing of the female bird.

He cut open the calamus of a feather,

To get in and hide.

Soon he heard the bell of the red deer.

In heavy fog,

It was nearly dawn,

The two giant birds were flapping their wings.

When they flew above the ocean,

---

① In Dai legend, ruohalilin is the biggest bird.

雌鸟感到身上发痒

她想抖一抖身子

让什么东西掉进海洋

雄鸟说："初一不杀生

十五不害命

明天是十五

请你把他饶恕"

The female felt itchy.

She tried to shake it off,

And throw it into the ocean.

The male said, "No killing on the first day[①],

Nor on the fifteenth day.

Tomorrow happens to be the fifteenth day,

So let him go."

---

① The first day refers to the first day of the lunar month. —Translator's note

第十一章 到了勐董板地方

Canto 11　Arriving at Mengdongban

乌云里出现了阳光

喃婼娜飞回到她的家乡

阳光铺满地

鲜花朝她开放

父母姐姐都解开心里的疙瘩

一个个都很高兴

公主回来了

正像宝剑插回剑鞘

叭团叫人齐放六门大炮

通知全城的人都为女儿祝贺

百姓都像过节一样

等待着拴线的时刻

叭团又拿一对金手镯给喃婼娜

他不愿意把派兵救她的事告诉她

他说："女儿啊

从此，你再也不要离开勐董板

"愿你常在父母身边

像小鸟一样快活

愿你不要再惹上祸端

好让爹妈多活几年"

While the sunlight penetrated through the dark clouds,

Nanruona flew back to her hometown,

Where there was abundant sunshine,

Where flowers were blooming for her.

The princess came back,

As if a sword was back in its sheath.

Her parents and sisters were pleased,

As if the knots in their hearts were untied.

Batuan gave orders to fire six salutes,

And informed all the people to celebrate.

Just like celebrating their festivals,

They were waiting for the moment to hold the ceremony.

Batuan brought another pair of gold bracelets to Nanruona.

He was unwilling to tell the truth that he had sent troops to rescue her.

So he said, "my daughter,

From now on, never leave home again."

"I wish you would stay with us forever,

I wish you are happy like a bird,

I wish you would stay away from any trouble,

So that your mother and I can live longer."

父亲把金镯带在她手上

两手闪闪发光

喃婼娜和以前一样美丽

黑色的眉毛发亮

两只眼睛水汪汪

就像"都拉"① 出现在眼前

慈祥的父母坐在她身边

姐姐们都围在她后面

问她捉她的猎人是谁

这些日子她怎么生活

喃婼娜又想起了召树屯

她说猎人是她的丈夫

他们就像鱼和水

他们好像星星和月亮

全家人都十分惊奇

猎人怎么就夺去了她的心

难道她不是兵马抢救回来

难道她只是回来探亲

---

① 都拉：天仙或美丽的神。

The gold bracelets were put on her wrists,

Shining and glittering.

Nanruona was as fair as ever,

Her eyebrows black and shiny,

Her eyes clear and sparkling,

As if Dula① descended from heaven.

Her loving parents were sitting beside her,

Her sisters standing behind.

They inquired about the hunter,

And her past life.

It made her recall her husband.

She said her husband was the hunter,

One was to the other what water was to fish,

Or what the moon was to the stars.

The whole family was amazed

At how the hunter could win her heart.

Was she not saved by the army?

Was she back just to visit her family?

---

① Dula was a fairy or nymph in legend.

喃婼娜又埋怨战争

战争拆散了他们

为了战争

召树屯率军出征

叭团吃了一惊

从头发到脚趾他都感到不安

难道那个勇敢善战的少年

就是喃婼娜的男人

要是真的把他杀了

岂不害了喃婼娜的一生

他的嘴唇轻轻颤动

眼光显露着惶惑不宁

召树屯走了九百九十九天

来到了一个城市

这就是勐董板地方

这就是喃婼娜的家乡

召树屯走近城外的"撒拉房"①

只见人们来来往往

———————————

① 撒拉房：傣族路边盖的一种供路人休息的房子。

Again she complained about the warfare

Which split them up.

Due to the war, Zhaoshutun

Had to lead the army and leave home.

Batuan was surprised.

He felt uncomfortable from head to toe.

He realized that the brave young man

In the battle was his son-in-law.

If he had killed that man,

He would have destroyed his daughter's life.

His lips were quivering.

His eyes looked uneasy.

After nine hundred and ninety-nine days,

Zhaoshutun came to another city.

It was Mengdongban,

Nanruona's hometown.

Outside the city he approached a hut①.

People came and went from it.

———————————

① A temporary shelter for people who pass by.

女人们穿着五彩的绸缎
身上的珠宝闪闪发光

召树屯走了三年
勐董板才过了三天
姑娘们用金锅挑水
准备为喃婼娜拴线

有一个姑娘叫喃新莎
她是喃婼娜的侍女
她挑着金锅走到井边
她是给喃婼娜挑水洗身

召树屯走向喃新莎的身边
他暗暗祈求天神
如果她是给喃婼娜挑水
求天神叫她提不起金锅

果然，喃新莎虽然用尽力气
用尽力气也不能把金锅提起
她抬头看见了召树屯
就请求他帮助一臂之力

召树屯帮她把金锅抬上肩

Women were in colorful satin.

The jewelry on their bodies shone.

Yet Zhaoshutun had traveled for three years,

Only three days had gone by in Mengdongban.

Girls were carrying water with pots of gold,

And preparing for the rite of tying a thread.

A girl, named Nanxinsha,

Was the maid of Nanruona.

She came to the well with a gold pot.

She was preparing the bath water for the princess.

Zhaoshutun came up to her.

He secretly prayed to God that

If she were the maid for Nanruona,

She would not be able to hold up the pot.

Indeed, Nanxinsha did not hold up the pot,

Even if she exerted all her strength.

She raised her head and saw Zhaoshutun,

And asked him for help.

Zhaoshutun helped her to put the pot on her shoulder,

他悄悄把金手镯放进锅里
他说："你是个好姑娘
你生得这样美丽"

姑娘满脸通红
心里却像吃了蜂蜜
她说："小伙子呀
你是一只会说话的鹦哥
我是一棵快枯的老树
请你不要拿我取乐

"你是长得这样漂亮
勐董板找不到你这样耀眼的太阳
我没有福气请你挑水
全城的百姓都正在奔忙"

召树屯又问道
"姑娘呀，你来来回回挑了这样多水
是不是像燕子衔泥
为自己筑窠"

喃新莎觉得很惊奇
"全城的人都知道喃婼娜回来
小伙子呀，难道你没有给她祝贺

In which he secretly put a gold bracelet.

He said, "You are a good maid,

And you have a pretty face."

Her face flushed with embarrassment,

Her heart was sweet as if she had just eaten honey.

She said, "Young man,

You are a honey-lipped parrot,

I am an old withering tree,

Please don't make fun of me."

"You are so handsome

That I have never met a shiny man like you.

I'm not fortunate enough to ask you to carry water for me.

All the people are busy in our city today."

Zhaoshutun then said,

"You go back and forth several times,

Like a swallow carrying bits of earth in her bill

To build her own nest."

Nanxinsha was surprised,

"Everyone knows that Nanruona is back,

Haven't you come to congratulate her?

我挑的水就是为她'洗福'①"

"姑娘啊

原来你挑的是仙水

你应该告诉喃婼娜举起手来

再把圣水从她头上冲下

这样她的福气就会更大"

喃新莎回去后依照他的话去做

当水从喃婼娜头上冲下

金手镯便落在她的手上

喃婼娜十分奇怪

为什么这只金手镯又回到她手中

她问喃新莎遇到了谁

来自何方

什么样子

什么姓名

喃新莎回答

"今天挑水不比平常

有一个年轻的小伙子

---

① 洗福：傣族的一种风俗，凡远离和久别归来的人，都要在家里用水洗澡，以示吉祥。

The water is for her Xifu[①]."

He replied, "Nice girl,

Now that you bring her the holy water,

Please tell her she should raise her arms

And pour the water down from her head.

So she would have better fortune."

Nanxinsha did what he said.

When the holy water was poured from her head,

The gold bracelet fell on Nanruona's hands.

She was curious

About why it had come back to her.

She asked Nanxinsha whom she came across,

Where he came from,

What he looked like,

What about his name.

Nanxinsha answered,

"It is an unusual day today.

I met a young man.

---

① Xifu is a Dai custom. It means taking a bath in order to get rid of misfortune and have good luck, especially for those who return home after being away a long time.

问我为什么挑水
又教了我这个办法"

喃婼娜又高兴又疑惑
难道丈夫真的来到
他是地上走来
还是天上飞来

喃婼娜急忙披上纱毯
向她的父母跑去
一面走一面流泪
一面揩眼泪一面叫喊

"阿爹阿妈啊
我的丈夫……他来了
喃新莎亲眼看见
他现在井边……"

叭团头人们都很惊奇
他们虽然心里感到怀疑
同时又派了大象来到井边
他们把召树屯接回宫殿

He asked why I fetched water

And taught me to do it in this way."

Nanruona felt excited and doubtful about

Whether her husband had come or not,

Whether he had come here on foot,

Or flew in.

Nanruona wrapped a scarf around her hurriedly,

And ran to her parents.

She wept while walking,

She cried while wiping tears.

"Father and mother,

My husband is coming.

Nanxinsha saw him herself.

Now he is right beside the well."

Batuan and the tribal chiefs were astonished.

They thought it was unbelievable,

So they sent an elephant for Zhaoshutun

To come to the palace.

第十二章 团圆

Canto 12　Reunion

叭团看见召树屯心里喜欢

年轻美丽一表人才

他摆开酒席

却不让他们夫妻见面

召树屯十分纳闷

两眼四处看望

送酒送菜的人来来往往

就是不见喃婼娜的面

喃婼娜啊

急得像火烧身

窗前望了后门瞧

为什么还不见召树屯进来

叭团举起酒杯

只把闲话问

"年轻的人，你是怎么来的

顺着大风呢

还是驾着白云

"你的父母在哪里

你的家乡是什么情形

为什么独自一人来

Batuan was delighted with Zhaoshutun,

Young and handsome.

He gave a feast,

Yet the young couple still did not meet.

Zhaoshutun was puzzled.

He looked around and searched

Everyone in the crowd.

Yet he couldn't find her.

Like an ant on a hot pan,

Nanruona also looked around

From the window to the door,

Anxiously waiting for her husband.

Batuan raised his glass of wine,

And asked Zhaoshutun some trivial questions,

"Young man, how did you get here?

Riding on clouds?

Or riding on the wind?

"Where are your parents?

What is your hometown like?

Why do you come alone?

你有什么本领"

召树屯回答一句转一下眼
到了勐董板地方
难道是喃婼娜故意不见
难道是丈人对他敷衍

召树屯跪在叭团面前
他请求得到饶恕
冒昧来到勐董板地方
只要求和喃婼娜见一面

叭团有意要看一看女婿的本领
让头人和百姓都来称赞召树屯
他传令用铁挡住道路
再把石头堆成石墙
第三层的石墙又钉上铁钉

他说："年轻的人
你能够一箭打开这道墙
喃婼娜就是你的妻子
我就把你招为女婿"

召树屯只好拿起弓箭

Do you have any special talent?"

Zhaoshutun answered his questions one by one,

And wondered

Whether she refused to see him on purpose,

Or his father-in-law played tricks on him.

Zhaoshutun knelt down before him,

And begged for pardon.

He explained the reason why he came,

And hoped to see Nanruona again.

Batuan wanted to see his talent.

The tribal chiefs and civilians were required to watch.

He ordered people to block the road with ironwork,

Pile up three stone walls,

And reinforce the third wall with iron nails.

Batuan said, "Young man,

If you can break them down with an arrow,

Nanruona will marry you,

And you will be my son-in-law."

Zhaoshutun held up his bow and arrows,

沉着地骑上马

像百鸟中飞来一只凤凰

四面的眼光都看着他

他拉起弓

马往前扑

风往后闪

箭响如雷鸣

三道墙全都崩开

百姓都"水！水！"地欢呼

没有人不称赞召树屯的本领

力气最大的是象

象不能推开石墙

召树屯以为就会见到喃婼娜

没有想到叭团又叫人搭了一个平棚

用布把四面遮住

上面还绣了许多花朵

中间挖了一千个眼睛一样大的小洞

他叫了九百九十九个姑娘陪着喃婼娜

每人都从棚里伸出一个手指

然后把召树屯叫到棚下

And mounted his horse.

The villagers gazed at him,

As if he was a phoenix among birds.

He drew the bow,

With the horse running forward,

And the wind blowing backward,

The arrows flew like thunder,

And all the three walls were cracked.

The villagers cheered and shouted, "Shui! Shui!"

They all praised him for his talent.

Even a powerful elephant

Couldn't push down these stone walls.

Zhaoshutun thought he could meet his wife now.

Unexpectedly Batuan ordered a shed to be set up,

Covered with a cloth on which

There were many flowers embroidered.

There were one thousand eye-size holes in the cloth.

Nine hundred and ninety-nine girls accompanied Nannuona.

Each of them was required to stretch a finger out of one hole.

Then Zhaoshutun was called over.

"年轻的人啊

如果你认不出喃婼娜的手指

就请你快点转回家

以后再也不要想念喃婼娜"

召树屯皱起了眉头

深山里捉鱼

还可以找到沟

一千个手指

像一千株藕芽

叫他选择哪一个

他绕着布棚走了一圈

一千个手指都看了一遍

其中有一个手指

像有一只萤火虫落在上边

这是玉石戒指

啊！不，这是喃婼娜爱情放出的光焰

他紧紧抓住了这个手指

这就是我的喃婼娜

头人百姓都为他欢呼

"Young man,

If you can not recognize her finger,

You have to go back

And forget her."

Zhaoshutun was stumped, frowning,

"It's easy to catch a fish in the mountains,

Because I can find a ditch.

One thousand fingers are just

Like one thousand sprouts of lotuses.

What can I do?"

He walked around the shed,

Examining the fingers one by one.

He focused his attention on a finger

On which there seemed to be a glowworm resting.

It seemed like a jade ring.

Oh! No, it must be the flame of her love.

He held it tightly.

He was certain it belonged to Nanruona.

The tribal chiefs and the villagers cheered,

叭团和他妻子

扶出了喃婼娜

百姓四面把他们围住

召树屯和喃婼娜

站在百姓的中间

就像千万匹绿叶中间

开放出两朵鲜红的玫瑰

头人和百姓都向他们朝拜

有的人献上好马和大象

有的人为他们祝福

从今后，永远不再分离……

Batuan and the Queen

Helped Nanruona out,

The crowd swarmed round them.

Zhaoshutun and Nanruona

Were standing in the middle,

As if two red roses were

Clustered round by millions of green leaves.

The tribal chiefs and their followers paid their respect to them.

Some people presented steeds and elephants.

Some sent greetings and blessings.

From then on, they would always be together.

About the Translators

Wu Xiangru is a professor of English in the School of Foreign Languages and Literature at Yunnan Normal University. His recent publications include: *An Analysis of New Words in Contemporary English* (Yunnan University Press, 2003), *English Academic Essay Writing and Research* (Yunnan University Press, 2004), and more than ten articles on translation strategies and literature. His research interests focus on English literary study and translation.

Wu Jiong is a lecturer of English in the Foreign Language Department at Chuxiong Normal University. Her recent publications include *A Study of Translation Skills and Practices on the Basis of Cross-cultural Communication* (Xinhua Publishing House, 2015), and some articles on translation strategies and translation teaching. Her research interests focus on literary translation, pedagogy and cross-cultural communication.

(Wu Jiong translated the whole poem into English. Wu Xiangru read the first draft and made corrections.)